"Get Back Here," Lee Commanded From The Bed.

Diana shook her head. "No. I'd better not."

He rose to stand behind her, resting his arms on her shoulders. She could feel his warm breath on the back of her neck.

"Don't my kisses please you anymore?" he asked. Without waiting for her to answer, he turned her around to face him and began to trace the outline of her lips with the tip of his tongue. "Is that what you don't like?" he murmured.

"Oh, yes," Diana gasped through the tremors that wracked her. "I simply hate that. You know I do."

"Mmm, I thought so. And you're not too keen on this, either, are you?" He began inflicting sweet torture on the place just below her ear, caressing her with the skill born of much practice.

"That's right," Diana sighed, trying not to abandon all self-restraint.

"Suppose I just keep on kissing you," Lee whispered, "until I get it right...."

Dear Reader:

Happy New Year! Now that the holiday rush is through you can sit down, kick off your shoes and open the cover of a Silhouette Desire.

As you might know, we'll be continuing the *Man of the Month* program through 1990. In the upcoming year look for men created by some of your favorite authors: Elizabeth Lowell, Annette Broadrick, Diana Palmer, Nancy Martin and Ann Major. Also, we'll be presenting Barbara Boswell's first-Desire-ever as a *Man of the Month*.

But Desire is more than the *Man of the Month*. Each and every book is a wonderful love story in which the emotional and the sensual go hand-in-hand. The book can be humorous or serious, but it will always be satisfying.

So whether you're a first-time reader or a regular, welcome to Desire 1990—I know you're going to be pleased.

Lucia Macro
Senior Editor

LUCY GORDON

met her husband-to-be in Venice, fell in love the first evening and got engaged two days later. After seventeen years they're still happily married and now live in England with their three dogs. For twelve years Lucy was a writer on an English women's magazine. She interviewed many of the world's most interesting men, including Warren Beatty, Richard Chamberlain, Roger Moore, Sir Alec Guiness and Sir John Gielgud.

In 1985 she won the *Romantic Times* Reviewers Choice Award for Outstanding Series Romance Author. She has also won a Golden Leaf Award from the New Jersey Chapter of the RWA and was a finalist in the RWA Golden Medallion contest in 1988.

One

"Bless you for coming to my rescue, Portia," Nigel Marriott declared theatrically. "How can I ever thank you?"

"By not calling me Portia," Diana Waldman replied promptly. "I detest it."

She flicked back a stray curl of soft brown hair and banished a minute speck of dust from her gray skirt. On courtroom days Diana always tried to look severe by pinning back her luxurious hair and wearing austere clothes. She was partly successful, but no amount of careful presentation could hide the beauty of her warm skin and dark brown eyes, or the charm of her smile.

At twenty-seven she had a reputation as a high-flyer in the legal world. Opposing counsels had been known to groan at the thought of facing her incisive mind and ruthless attack. Diana rarely visited the lower courts where minor cases were tried. She was only there this morning to do a favor for Hugh Marriott, a dear friend whose younger brother was in a mess of his own making. Hugh was a banker, a man of solid worth. If Diana occasionally found him a touch pompous, she also knew him to have a kind heart. How he'd come to possess a brother as crassly vulgar as young Nigel was a mystery to her.

"I know this kind of trivial case is beneath your notice these days," Hugh had said with a deprecating smile. "But I'd be endlessly grateful if you'd help Nigel out."

She'd agreed at once. She was deeply fond of their mother who'd been kind to her in her motherless teens and was bedridden now. Besides, Diana could never resist a plea for help.

Now she was half regretting it. Nigel was more exasperating than usual this morning. The reckless scamp seemed incapable of understanding that he was in the wrong. "If I'm going to help you, you've got to behave yourself," she told him severely. "If you weren't such an irresponsible young idiot, we wouldn't be here at all."

Nigel looked aggrieved. "I couldn't help it. The police harassed me and I hope you're going to complain about it."

"The police didn't harass you," Diana explained patiently. "They very properly pointed out that your car was causing an obstruction. You should have had the sense to shut up and move it before they noticed your registration was also out of date. What you should *not* have done was argue with the officer and then assault him."

"Assault him? I only trod on his toe," Nigel yelped.

"Legally that's an assault." Diana's eyes sparkled with annoyance. "Now look, your only hope is complete abjection. You do not waste the court's time blithering on about police harassment. You grovel. You abase yourself. And if we're very lucky you may get off with a caution. Is that clear?"

"Yes ma'am." Mopping his brow, Nigel sank back into a seat next to Hugh. "You didn't tell me she was going to lecture me like a headmistress," he complained.

Hugh frowned at him. "You should have expected it from Lord Justice Waldman's granddaughter," he said unsympathetically. "He was one of the most feared men ever to sit on the bench—totally scrupulous, utterly just and completely ruthless."

"You mean that glorious creature is a chip off the old block?"

"In some ways, yes—as you've just discovered. Now stay quiet. They're about to call us into court."

They all filed in, and when the preliminaries were over Diana delivered a short speech emphasizing her client's remorse for an uncharacteristic aberration. The magistrate promptly launched into a homily on the need to make an example of the hooligan elements in society. Hugh groaned.

"It's all right," Diana murmured. "Mr. Rogers is a dear old boy. When he talks tough it's always the prelude to coming down easy."

Hugh accepted her estimate without question. Diana had been raised by her awesome grandfather since the age of ten, and she knew just about everyone in the legal world. A few moments later the magistrate fulfilled her prophecy by letting Nigel off with a fine.

"That was heavy going," the young man complained to Diana. "I thought you were a wizard who could perform miracles."

"She did perform a miracle you ungrateful worm," Hugh said. "She prevented you from making things any worse. Clear out." When Nigel had made a hasty departure he said, "Thank you. It'll be such a weight off Mother's mind. I suppose this hasn't helped my chances of persuading you to marry me?"

"It hasn't helped or hindered them, Hugh. When I decide it won't be because of your brother."

"I wish you'd decide quickly and make it 'yes.' Mother's dying to welcome you into the family."

"Give me a little more time."

"Of course, my dear. In the meantime, will you have dinner with me tonight?"

"I'm afraid I can't. It's one of my nights for going to the refuge."

"You mean that church crypt full of smelly old tramps? Why on earth do you bother with them? I know your passion for lame dogs, but isn't that going a bit far?"

"I don't think so," Diana said. She spoke lightly but an air of reserve settled over her, signaling that the subject was closed.

"We'd better get out," he said. "The next case is due."

Diana finished gathering her papers and turned to go, but she paused a moment to look at the man being led in. He was in his thirties, with a lean, unshaven face that bore a number of scratches and bruises. He was dressed in an old, shabby suit, torn in several places, and his eyes were sunk as though he hadn't eaten or slept properly for some time. He stared straight ahead of him in either defiance or despair. Diana looked around for his counsel, but couldn't see anyone who seemed responsible for him.

"Come on, Diana," Hugh urged.

"No, you go ahead. I want to stay for a moment."

Hugh followed the direction of her eyes. "Don't start feeling sorry for *that* one."

"Do you know him?"

"No, but I can tell a bad character when I see one. Let's go."

"I'm staying here," she said firmly.

The man had reached the dock and stood there, staring sullenly at the floor. Diana sat down, watching him.

Mr. Rogers, the magistrate, looked through his paper, then said, "I believe the next case is Lee—Lee who? I don't seem to have a last name here."

A policeman stood up and said, "We've been unable to obtain the prisoner's last name."

"What is your name?" Mr. Rogers demanded.

The man looked at him bitterly. "You've got it there. My name's Lee."

"Lee what?"

The prisoner was silent.

"You must have a surname. What is it?"

Silence.

"You're not making things any better for yourself by this attitude," the magistrate said severely.

Lee raised his head and looked the magistrate square in the face while a bitter expression twisted his lips. "You're going to send me to jail anyway, so why don't you just get on with it?" he demanded ironically.

"I'll ignore that remark," Mr. Rogers told him. "I see you're charged with being drunken and disorderly, disturbing the peace, resisting arrest and assaulting a police officer. Who represents you?''

The policeman spoke again. "The accused has refused all offers of help.''

"This is most unsatisfactory. He must have someone to defend him.''

"As though it made any difference,'' Lee jeered.

Diana rose. "If it please the court, I should like to represent the accused,'' she said.

"I said I don't want anyone,'' Lee snapped.

"Be quiet,'' the magistrate reproved him. "Miss Waldman, I'm most obliged for your kind offer. The case will be deferred to give you time to confer with your client. Take the prisoner downstairs.''

A policeman took him by the arm. The man tried to shake him off, but another policeman appeared and the two of them half urged and half shoved him out of the courtroom.

"Diana, have you gone mad?'' Hugh exclaimed. "Anyone can see he's an incorrigible brute.''

"If he's such a brute, where did he get all those nasty bruises?'' she demanded. "You didn't seen any bruises on the police officer, did you?''

"He resisted arrest and they had to subdue him.''

"There's something about this business that isn't right, Hugh, and I'm going to find out what it is.''

"But you heard him. He doesn't want your help.''

"He may not want it, but he's going to get it.''

She hurried down to the cells below the court and found herself confronted by a large policeman who looked thoroughly displeased by the turn of events. "I'm Constable Horton. If I were you, miss, I wouldn't waste my time on him,'' he said. "He's a bad lot.''

"Kindly get out of my way," she said firmly. "I wish to speak with my client."

Reluctantly he led her to a cell, then opened the door. The prisoner was inside, standing by the window. He regarded her with indifference as she came in and set her things on the little table. "Thank you," she said to the policeman. "Don't let me detain you."

"It's better if I stay, miss. This one's violent."

Diana's lips tightened with anger. "I demand to be left alone with my client," she snapped.

Constable Horton shrugged and went out. As the door clanged shut, she turned to find Lee leaning against the wall, his arms folded, watching her with a look of derision. "Why don't you just go away and stop playing Lady Bountiful?" he asked.

"I'm not *playing* at anything. It matters that you should have someone acting on your behalf."

"I can do that for myself."

"If the sample I've just seen is anything to go by, you're pretty useless at it. You'd end up going to jail for contempt of court."

"So what? It's a bed for the night, isn't it? Prisons have roofs that keep out the rain."

"You talk as if you know all about prisons."

"I've been in a few," he said laconically.

She looked at the papers. "There's nothing here about your having a previous record."

"How could there be? They don't know my name."

"I see," Diana said wryly. "Then perhaps I'd better not ask any more."

"You'd better not ask anything. I want you to go, right now."

She had seated herself, and as he spoke Lee moved forward, then put his hands on the table, leaning over her. She guessed he was trying to intimidate her, but instead of apprehension she was acutely aware of an air of intense masculinity that flowed from his body. He had a clean smell, not like the tramp he looked, which meant that for all his bitter talk he still had some self-respect, and there was a chance she could reach him.

She looked up and found herself gazing into the most beautiful pair of dark brown eyes she'd ever seen. He sounded English, but his looks could have been Mediterranean. His black hair had a hint of curl, his skin was almost swarthy and his mouth was shapely and expressive. It was slightly crooked and looked as if at other times it might laugh easily. Now the lips were twisted as though he found her entertaining. "You're wasting your time," she told him. "I'm staying."

The derision about his mouth changed to a grin of genuine amusement, and he seated himself on the other side of the table. "I should warn you I haven't any money," he said.

"I don't want any."

"You mean you're doing this out of the goodness of your heart? Does it give you a lift to know you picked someone out of the gutter and gave him 'a fair deal'?"

Diana flushed. "Does it give *you* a lift to turn yourself into a martyr?" she snapped.

He raised his eyebrows in appreciation of her comeback. *"Touché,"* he conceded after a moment.

"Now perhaps we can start. My name is Diana Waldman."

"Waldman? No relation to Lord Justice Waldman?"

"He was my grandfather," Diana said, looking at him curiously.

Lee gave a long whistle.

"What do you know about him?" she asked

A cautious look came into his eyes. "Only what every criminal knows. He was the one you prayed not to find facing you from the bench. What's his granddaughter doing in such a lowly court? Didn't Granddad's connections get you something better than this?"

Diana spoke in a hard voice. "Since you ask—no, my grandfather wouldn't have dreamed of using his connections to advance his relatives, and I wouldn't have dreamed of asking him to. I don't have to be here. I have plenty of work in the High Court, work which I earned for myself, but I came to help a friend and stayed to help *you*."

"Going slumming, huh?"

"Whatever you call it," she declared, gathering her things and rising, "it was the biggest mistake of my life. Goodbye. You can send yourself to jail in your own way."

She had reached the door and was about to call the constable when a sudden burst of common sense washed over her like a cold shower. He'd set out to goad her into leaving, and she'd fallen for it. A look at his grinning face confirmed it. Diana walked back to the table and sat down, furious with herself for falling into his trap, but even more for losing her self-control. "As I was saying," she resumed, "my name is Diana Waldman. Since you won't reveal your last name, I'll have to call you Lee."

"I'll call you Diana."

"You'll call me Miss Waldman."

"You evidently believe in preserving a proper distance," he said ironically.

"I believe in keeping things professional. Now, I want to know everything that happened."

"You're very used to giving orders, aren't you, Diana? Don't you ever say 'please,' or do you reserve that for those you consider your equals?"

She took a long breath, refusing to be provoked. "Will you *please* tell me what happened?"

He shrugged. "Drunk and disorderly. I was sleeping on the embankment with a group of others. It's warmer that way, and healthier too."

"Healthier?"

"You get familiar with one another's fleas and develop a kind of immunity," he said, regarding her innocently.

At the word fleas Diana couldn't resist a quick look down at herself and an involuntary shudder that prompted Lee to shout with laughter. She realized he'd been goading her again, and she made a resolution not to fall for his tricks a third time. It shouldn't be difficult. In court she was known for her ability to stay cool despite all provocation from an opposing counsel or an awkward judge.

"You were sleeping on the embankment," she repeated, writing it down. In fact her powerful memory made note taking unnecessary, but it was a way of not looking at him. She didn't want to see the disconcerting gleam of laughter in his eyes. There was something about this situation that was all wrong. She was used to helping down and outs, and to being in control during their consultation. But she wasn't in control now. This man was dangerous in a way that had nothing to do with physical violence.

"I got into a fight with some of my fellow tramps. I had a cardboard box that was somewhat better than their cardboard boxes, and in our world these things matter in a way you couldn't possibly imagine. When he tried to take it off me I resisted, it all got worse from there. The next thing I knew the police came along. I told them not to interfere in a private dispute but they didn't see it that way. So here I am."

"Just you? Weren't any of the others arrested too?"

He shrugged. "I guess they were wise enough not to argue with the police."

"It says here you resisted arrest. How did you get those bruises on your face?"

"I told you, fighting."

"With the police?"

"What does it matter?" he said wearily.

"If the police knocked you about, I want to know," she insisted.

His mouth twisted in bitter sarcasm. "Why? Because you're a crusader against the police?"

"I'm no such thing."

"I think you are. I know your kind of lawyer. As far as you're concerned all coppers are pigs and all villains are saints. That's why you took me up, isn't it? Because I had some bruises that gave you an excuse to accuse the police of brutality."

Diana frowned, puzzled by a note of bitterness in his voice. She said. "If that was true—which it isn't—it would make me more useful to you, wouldn't it?"

"No, because I have more self-respect than to let myself be used as your cannon fodder. Look, we both know what the outcome will be. Jail, then back to the embankment."

"And another arrest? Is that what you want?"

He shrugged. "It's how hundreds live, but a Waldman wouldn't know about that."

"Of course I know. I see plenty of the seamy side of life."

"Oh yes, I know how you see it, cut up into neat half hour segments and then on to the next client. You see it, but you don't have to live it. There's always an escape route for you."

He stopped, waiting for her to come back at him with a defensive retort, but instead she leaned back in her chair, her expression abstracted. "Yes, I suppose that's true," she said in a brooding voice. "I often wonder what becomes of people after they've passed out of my life. I worry about the ones I've failed. How do they survive in prison? And the others, the ones I get off—" She fell silent.

"If you get them off, why worry about them?" he asked.

"Because the verdict isn't the final curtain," she said. "Not for them. They have to go home and live their lives as changed people, sometimes the experience they get in court wounds them so much that they can't cope anymore. I prosecuted a man for rape once. He defended himself by denigrating the woman—'She wanted it,' that kind of thing. Her husband started the trial with his arm around her. When it finished, he was sitting six inches away with his arms tight at his side."

"What was the verdict?" Lee asked.

"Guilty, I'm proud to say. The man was sent down for seven years. But the damage was done. As that couple walked from the court, you could see the husband keeping his distance. That was a year ago. For all I know the experience may have destroyed their marriage." She sighed. "Sometimes the law can be a dreadful blunt instrument that does almost as much harm as the original crime.''

''You're the first lawyer I've ever heard admit that,'' Lee said, looking at her curiously.

His words startled her into an admission of what she'd said. She'd been speaking as she might have done to a colleague, not a vagrant. But he was no ordinary vagrant. The sharp intelligence in his face proclaimed that. Just the same, this wasn't the time or place to be talking about herself. It was absurd that she'd let him lead her into doing so. ''Let's get back to your problem,'' she said firmly.

''My only problem is a nosy lawyer who doesn't know when she's not wanted.''

''Anyone would think you preferred to go to jail,'' Diana said crossly.

''I've told you before, it's warm and dry in there.''

''I know a better place to be warm and dry.'' Diana took a small notebook from her purse, scribbled something on it and pushed it over the table to him.

''St. Mark's Crypt, Verney Street,'' he read without touching the notebook. ''What's that supposed to mean?''

''It's a refuge where people can go for a meal and somewhere to stay the night. The food's good, although the bedding's a bit primitive.''

''You mean it's not up to the standard of a prison cell?''

''It's a sight better than the embankment,'' she retorted. ''What's more, the police don't trouble us.''

''Us?'' His lips twitched. ''You mean *you* sleep there?''

''I help out a couple of evenings a week. Keep the address and come to us instead of the embankment.''

He gave her a strange look. "Do you do this for everyone?"

Diana was suddenly self-conscious, as though he'd looked into her and seen that she was drawn to him in a special way. It was no use telling herself that he was just another client. This man was different. She didn't know how, but she had a disturbing inclination to find out. "I simply try to help people if they seem to need it," she muttered.

"That's a mug's game," he said roughly. "You just encourage people to take advantage of you." He got up and strode impatiently about the cell. "Look at the risk you take being shut in here with me. They warned you I'm violent."

"But I don't believe you're violent."

He gave a wolfish grin and came to lean over her, putting one hand on each side of the chair back so that she was trapped. "Are you so sure of that?" he asked softly.

The sense of danger was there again, increased a thousandfold. It emanated from him like waves of heat, making hectic thoughts scurry across Diana's brain. The breath had caught in her throat, forcing her to fight to speak normally. "If you're trying to demonstrate that you're stronger than I am, there's no need," she told him. "I already know it, and so what?"

"So what? So I could do anything I liked before they had time to reach you. Always assuming I let you cry out."

"I'm not going to cry out," she said firmly. "I'm not afraid of you." But something else was making her heart thump.

"Then why won't you look at me, Diana?"

She did so and immediately regretted it. His face was very close to hers, the beautifully molded lips just a tantalizing inch away. She knew what he'd do if she tried to raise the alarm. "Let me go," she whispered.

She could hear that his breathing had changed. It had a ragged edge now, as though the same disturbance that troubled her had affected him. His eyes held a surprised look. "Make me," he challenged her.

Diana made a determined movement to stand, as though trying to break out of a forbidden spell. Lee backed off just enough to let her get to her feet, but then he tightened his arms about her and pulled her close to him. She felt the hard, warm length of his body against hers and had just enough time to realize that he was a good deal stronger than his battered appearance suggested before his mouth came down on hers.

For a moment she was aware of nothing but shock. She stood rigid in his arms, feeling his lips hard on hers, and the slight tickling of his beard stubble. Then there was a change. His mouth softened, relaxed, and eased its pressure. He began to use it with subtle power, teasing her own lips with persuasive movements. A thrill of apprehension went through her at the realization that something about the world had slipped askew.

This was a tramp, a down and out, one of the forlorn strays whose hands she often held comfortingly in her own capable ones. Yet he was kissing her with the ruthless confidence of a man who didn't need her help because he could cope with the world on his own terms. That was the message that was reaching her through his firm, skillful lips. And even worse was the way she was responding. Despite her anger a small flame of pure pleasure had come alive within her, and every seductive caress threatened to fan it higher.

Diana made a convulsive movement, but he held her easily. Something alarming was happening to her, and she knew she must stop this before her professional self was consumed by the treacherous, sweet warmth that was beginning to possess her. She didn't want to stop. She wanted to stay where she was and let the fire rise in great engulfing flames. She was a strong-minded woman, but suddenly it was so hard to be strong.

She made a last effort, trying to escape his mouth by twisting sideways, but he slipped his hand behind her head, twining his fingers in her hair so that it came loose, cascading about her shoulders. "Let me go at once," she said breathlessly.

She had a vision of his dark eyes blazing down at her with a strange hypnotic light. "You should have gone when you had the chance," he said in a grating voice, before locking his mouth on hers again.

This time he kissed her harder, with a kind of suppressed fierceness. He'd been venturing cautiously during the first kiss. Now he was asserting himself with a dominating force that made nonsense of their respective positions. Diana felt his tongue flicking against her lips, commanding her to open them. She fought him silently as long as she could, but he had her on the run and he knew it. She had no power to resist his tongue as it forced its way between her lips.

He was tracing a path around the soft inner flesh, setting off electric impulses that sparkled brilliantly through her bringing her whole body to life. He *must* stop. He was turning her into a different person, and she didn't like it. But at the same time she never wanted him to stop, and the different person beckoned at the door of a vivid new life.

She couldn't repress the soft moan that broke from her. It was part pleasure, part eager consent to the beautiful visions his kiss opened up. She managed to bend her arms enough to cling to him. She was giddy, lost in a haze where nothing existed but their two selves. She felt him draw back, and when she opened her eyes she saw that he was looking down at her with a dazed expression. His breath was coming in short gasps through his parted lips, and when he spoke his voice was hoarse. *"Diana..."* he said with a kind of astonished urgency.

"Yes..." she murmured.

This time her lips were burning in sweet anticipation as she watched him bend toward her. His touch sent the fire roaring through her, coaxing her passion to surface from the depths of her soul. But the beauty was abruptly snatched away. Through the haze she was dimly aware of a clang as the cell door was thrown open. Then Lee was hauled off her by two policemen and thrust back against the far wall.

"Are you all right, miss?" Constable Horton demanded.

"Yes, thank you," Diana said, trying not to let her voice shake. As reality came rushing back, she was filled with shame and horror at her own behavior. She forced herself to meet Lee's eyes. "You were right. I'm wasting my time."

"You'll know better than to come back, won't you?" he jeered as she walked out.

The two constables left the cell with her, locking the door behind them. She frantically pinned her hair back into its usual neat style, and Horton escorted her back into the court, where she made a formal apology and explained that she was unable to represent the prisoner after all. Then she departed with her head high, and only a slight flush on her cheeks betraying that anything unusual had happened.

Horton saw her go before returning to the cell and letting himself in. This time he didn't bother to lock the door. "That was a close call," he observed. His manner to Lee was noticeably different, almost friendly. "The last thing we want is any smart lawyers showing how thin our case against you really is."

Lee grunted agreement. His manner was also very different. "You should have made it more convincing from the start."

"Well, she's gone now. You'll be back in court in a few minutes, and with any luck you'll get sent away for three months. Two months with good behavior. With parole it could even be shorter, assuming you get Sammy to open up about the Corby gang."

"It's all set up with the prison governor?"

"Yes, he knows you're police. There's a spare bunk waiting for you in Sammy's cell. You win his confidence, he thinks he's talking to a fellow villain and we collar the whole gang."

An hour later Lee was driven away in a prison van to start his sentence. As the door of the jail thundered shut behind him, he gave himself a shake.

Into his mind came the memory of Diana saying, "I often wonder what becomes of people after they've passed out of my life." In a short but distinguished career he'd often been inside jails to interview prisoners, but he'd never wondered what life was like for those who had to stay behind when he left. Now he was discovering, and it was hateful.

At the desk he was stripped of all his possessions, but he managed to hang on to one thing. Late that night, lying on the top bunk in the darkness. Lee eased a leg out of bed and retrieved a scrap of paper from between his toes. It was a bit soggy because he'd had to place it there before the shower, but by the light from the small barred window he could still read the name of St. Mark's Crypt.

For a moment he could see Diana again, feel her soft body against his and the honey taste of her lips. The memory made his body throb with delightful heat. But frustration soon cooled his musings when he remembered how long he might be here. An involuntary groan broke from him, as he privately lamented his fate.

Sammy's voice reached him from below. "They all feel like that the first night. Prison's a real—" He finished with a profanity.

"Yes," Lee said with feeling. "It is."

Two

Diana parked her car in a side street and got out, pulling her jacket around her against the cold night air. She ran the few yards to St. Mark's, ducking her head into the wind. As she turned the corner she could see a couple of tramps making their way hurriedly down the stairs beside the old church. She hailed them by name, and they waved a greeting.

Downstairs there was welcome warmth and light. And there was Gavin, one of the young pastors who ran the place, dispensing tea from an urn. Diana joined the queue, and receiving her plastic cup gratefully.

St. Mark's was seven hundred years old, a well-built stone edifice that looked as if it could stand for another seven hundred years. The crypt was large, its ceiling supported by stone arches between which some blankets had been strung, creating an illusion of privacy. Mattresses were strewn around the floor, most of them already occupied by shabbily dressed men and women who seemed able to sleep through the noise of their neighbors.

"It's nice to see you again so soon," Gavin observed.

"So soon? I always come twice a week," Diana said, surprised.

"I know. But recently you've been coming three or four times a week. I'm not knocking it. We're glad of the help."

Diana let it go with a noncommittal remark. She was startled to realize that Gavin was right. She had stepped up her visits lately.

It was two months since the incident at the magistrate's court. Diana had left without waiting to discover Lee's fate, but the following morning she'd called the court and learned of his three month sentence. She'd ordered herself to forget the whole thing, but for once her superbly disciplined mind seemed to have gotten out of control. The memory of Lee obstinately presented itself at unexpected moments. This morning she'd pulled off a stunning victory in a case no one had expected her to win. The court had erupted with excitement. Even the judge had smiled. Diana had stood amid the plaudits, wondering if Lee had been released to go in search of another cardboard box. So far there was no sign of him at the crypt.

"Some old friends in tonight," Gavin observed, "and some new ones."

"I'll start getting their names," Diana said.

This wasn't the easy job it sounded. Newcomers ranged from the mentally vague and the tipsy who couldn't remember their names, to those who made a fiendish game out of making her guess. Then there were the superarticulate who proffered a stream of names, none of which was likely to be the right one.

"Be careful," Gavin advised her. "Some of the newcomers look as if they might turn nasty. It's odd, but we've been having quite a few of those recently."

"They all look like that at first," she said easily. "But most of them turn out to be gentle souls who just want someone to take an interest in them."

Finishing her tea, Diana started wandering between the lines of mattresses, greeting familiar faces, looking for strange ones. Her professional colleagues would hardly have recognized her now. The severely elegant clothes she wore to court had been replaced by jeans and chunky wool sweater. She had pulled her hair free of pins, letting it swing loose, making her look younger. Her shoes were flat and serviceable, and instead of the delicate little gold watch she normally wore, her wrist sported a cheap plastic timepiece.

She settled for a few minutes beside an old woman who launched into a rambling tale that Diana found hard to follow. But she tried, knowing that the only kindness anyone could do Kate now was to listen. She became aware of a man she hadn't seen before standing nearby, watching her with a slack-mouthed grin. He was younger and fitter looking than the men who usually found their way in here. One thing was certain, she didn't like the look of him. When at last she rose to go, he tried to take her arm, but she instinctively twisted away. "My name's Jake," he leered, blasting her with beer fumes. "Aren't you going to be nice to me too, darling?"

"No," she said firmly. "You don't need it, and there are plenty of people here who do."

"Now I call that unkind," Jake said thickly and made a lunge for her, but Diana sidestepped him by hooking her foot neatly at the back of his knee, causing him to sit down with a thump. A roar of appreciative laughter went up from around her. The noise seemed to arouse a man lying comatose in a corner, inducing him to slowly open an eye to see what the disturbance was. When he saw Diana he became very still.

He watched her coming closer, telling himself he ought to turn away before she recognized him, but postponing the moment until at last her eyes met his even though he knew it was too late. "Lee," Diana said, coming toward him and dropping on one knee. "So you did come here."

"Clear off," he muttered thickly. "Can't a fellow sleep in peace?"

The smell of cheap whisky assailed her, but she pressed on, undaunted by his condition. He had several days' growth of beard and his eyes were dark and sunken. "When did they release you?" she asked.

"Yesterday—last week—tomorrow—I don't know," he snarled. "What does it matter?"

As she leaned over him, her glorious hair swung down until it brushed his face. "Have you had anything to eat?"

"No," he growled, "and I don't want anything."

Lee closed his eyes, pretending he was no longer aware of her, but through a tiny gap in his eyelids he was able to watch as she rose to her feet and took a step back, colliding with Jake who'd come up behind her. "Don't bother with that bloke," Jake urged her. "Why don't you get *me* something to eat and we'll have it together, cozy like."

"I haven't any time," she said impatiently, trying to push him aside. But she'd lost the advantage of surprise this time, for Jake stood his ground, boldly placing a beefy hand on her breast.

"Then make ti—" The rest was lost as Lee's fist caught Jake on the jaw and sent him flying. Lee had sprung to his feet with incredible speed and now he stood there, all traces of drunken stupor gone, his hands still balled, and for a moment his sharp eyes met Diana's. Then his alertness seemed to desert him, he staggered, collapsing with his arm around her like a puppet whose strings had gone slack. But she was no longer deceived. Despite the whisky smell, Lee was stone cold sober.

"What are you playing at?" she whispered indignantly into his ear.

"Never mind that now," he muttered. His voice became blurred again. "I'm gonna pass out—blind drunk." He tried to sink away from her, by slumping to the ground, but she held on to him grimly.

"Like hell you are!" she snapped.

"Well, keep it to yourself," he growled in her ear.

"Not unless you tell me what's going on."

"All right. Let's get out of here. Pretend you're supporting me."

Together they weaved to the exit. When they were outside, Diana would have pushed him away but he gripped her, muttering, "No explanations here. Someone might be watching. Where's your car?"

Diana wondered if she'd gotten tangled up with a madman. She couldn't see anyone watching them, but she made a play of supporting him around the corner. "I don't know what game you're playing, but I feel very foolish," she grumbled.

"Just do as I say," he replied in a low voice.

"Who are you giving orders to?"

"Quit arguing."

When they reached the car Lee seemed to collapse against it. Once Diana opened the passenger door, he fell into the seat. She got behind the wheel and started up, her face grim.

Lee glanced behind him to see if they were being followed, but to his relief the dark street was deserted. He was furious with himself for what he'd just done. To risk blowing his cover just to protect this maddening woman was the worst kind of unprofessionalism. He was also furious with her for making it happen. "Look . . ." he began.

"Save it!" she ordered him. "You can tell me everything when we get home."

"I'm not going home with you."

"Oh yes you are. You're not leaving until I know what's going on." She could have screamed with vexation when she remembered how she'd pitied him.

Lee ground his teeth but said nothing. There was no time now to explain that he didn't want the men he was watching to follow and discover where she lived. He'd seen her safely away from the shelter, now he must leave her as soon as possible. To his relief the car was slowing for a set of traffic lights, giving him a chance to escape. "Thanks for the ride," he said. "I'll explain another time. Go straight on home without stopping and don't go back to that place."

He grasped the handle on the passenger door, but nothing happened. He tried again, pushing on the door, but it stayed firmly in place. "You're wasting your time," Diana told him. "I have a master lock on my side that secures every door in the car."

"Then kindly unlock this door."

"Oooh no! You owe me some explanations, and you're coming home with me to give them."

The car was moving again, and they'd reached a more crowded part of town. Diana was weaving in and out of traffic, traveling at a fast clip. It would have been too dangerous to wrestle with her for the lock, so Lee had no choice but sit there fuming. "You don't know what you've gotten yourself into," he growled.

"That's what you're going to tell me, and it had better be good."

Before long they had left the shabby part of town behind them and were driving through a leafy suburb. Now and then Lee glanced behind them but when he was unable to see anything suspicious, he began to relax. Once he stopped to take a look at Diana's profile as she sat with her eyes fixed on the road ahead. She was as beautiful and gracefully aristocratic as a thoroughbred racehorse, he thought, admiring her delicately determined chin. It occurred to him that some men might be reluctant to tangle with this lady, but no one had ever accused Lee of lacking courage. He was looking forward to it.

At last they turned onto a tree-lined road. All the houses were large, set well back from the pavements, with sweeping drives and covered porches, and Diana swung into one of these drives. In the beams from the headlights Lee saw that they'd reached an imposing Victorian edifice. A plaque proclaimed it to be Wendle House. It looked as if it had been built by a nineteenth-century merchant grown fat on trade, aspiring to more socially exalted circles but uncertain how to go about it. It was a strange house for the vibrantly modern young woman beside him.

Diana picked up the car phone and dialed. "Okay Martin, I'm back," she said at last. "Open up."

Martin. Lee mulled over the name, trying to decide if it sounded like a husband or lover, not liking the idea of either prospect.

The garage door began to rise, revealing a large interior with the lights already on. Diana drove inside, waited until the door was lowered again, then unlocked the car doors. "You can get out now," she said.

An elderly man had appeared in the doorway that connected the garage to the main house and stood on the threshold like an avenging angel. "What time do you call this to be getting back?" he demanded.

"Quit nagging," Diana told him amiably, kissing his cheek. She stood aside for Lee to pass into the house. "This way."

"You needn't herd me like a sheepdog," he grumbled. "I won't try to escape again."

"Very wise. Otherwise I'd have to set Martin onto you, and he's a terror." She exchanged an impish smile with the elderly man.

"I'll remember that," Lee promised.

"I see you've brought more riffraff home with you," Martin said, looking at Lee with disapproval. "Is this one staying long?"

"No. Only until I'm ready to throw him out," Diana said. She led the way into a large kitchen. Deep red flagstones covered the floor, and gleaming copper pots hung about the walls. A woman stood at the sink with her back to them. At first Lee thought she must be quite young. She had a lean, wiry figure, her dark hair was caught back in a ribbon at her neck, and she wore a patchwork skirt and a red embroidered peasant blouse. But then she turned and he saw she was elderly. Her face was hollow-cheeked and had a worn look as though at some time she'd known a lot of suffering, but her brilliant blue eyes were the eyes of a survivor. She surveyed Lee with humor, sniffing the air significantly. "Coffee," she said. "Sober you up."

"He's perfectly sober, Vita," Diana said tersely.

"Doesn't smell sober. Stinks of whisky."

"Yes, but he hadn't been drinking it." She turned to Lee. "Have you?"

"No, I just splashed some over my clothes," he admitted.

"More fool you to waste good whisky," Martin mourned.

Vita was pouring mugs of coffee. Lee wondered how she and Martin were related to Diana. Grandparents on her mother's side, perhaps? Certainly their air of raffishness ruled them out of the Waldman side of the family. "Supper's nearly ready," Vita said.

"Thanks. We just have enough time to talk first." Diana indicated the door. "Come on."

She walked ahead and Lee followed, clutching the coffee Vita had pressed into his hands. The smell of it assailed his nostrils, making him giddy with its perfection. Since his release he'd been living his tramp cover night and day, and could hardly remember his last proper meal. To increase his torture the kitchen was filled with delectable smells that he was regretfully going to have to walk away from.

Diana led him into a spacious room lined with books. Despite its size it had a cozy appearance. A coal fire burned in the fireplace, before which lay a huge dog of indeterminate ancestry. Rag rugs were scattered over the polished floor, and hunting prints covered the white walls.

An eight-foot-long sofa dominated the room. It contained a bespectacled young man engrossed in a book, with a cat asleep over his feet. The newcomer looked Lee up and down without curiosity, then said, "Hello, Di."

"Hello, Clive. Be a dear and vanish, would you? I have some urgent fighting to do and I don't want any of you to come in, no matter what you hear."

"She means you're to ignore my screams for help," Lee said. The youth grinned, then took his leave.

When they were alone Diana confronted him. "Now, let's hear it. Remember, I've heard every unlikely story that's going."

"Leaving aside the question of whether I owe you an explanation—" he began.

"Whether you—? What kind of man indulges in that kind of play-acting? You let me think you were so drunk you were practically comatose. But you moved fast enough when it suited you."

"To help you, yes. It's luck I wasn't expecting gratitude, isn't it?"

"Don't change the subject. You splashed that whisky over yourself for effect. No one in real need would waste it like that, it was all an elaborate con. But why? Does it give you a thrill to look at how the other half lives?" Diana stopped and a look of utter scorn came over her face. "My God," she breathed. "I know what you are. You're a welfare spy. Your bosses sent you down there to see if you could trap some little old lady who might be getting fourpence more than the law says she's entitled to. Of all the lowdown—"

"Will you hush up?" he said, raising his voice and scowling. "You're quite wrong. The fact is I'm a policeman."

She stared. "So now the police care about what those poor old folk get? That's even worse."

"Will you get it into your head that I'm not trying to trap any of your friends?" Lee snapped. "I don't care what welfare pays them. I hope it's as much as possible. I hope they've all got two identities and claim three times on every one of them. Is that clear enough?"

Diana's eyes narrowed suspiciously. "If you're trying to trap me into an admission—"

He groaned. "Give me patience. I am *not* after your tramp friends. The men I want are much bigger fish and engaged in something extremely dangerous."

"In the refuge?" she queried skeptically.

He gave a bark of laughter. "I should thank you for putting me on to that place. It was the thing that convinced my cellmate that I could be trusted."

"Your cellmate?" Indignation burned in Diana's eyes as the realization dawned on her. "The day we met—it was a put-up job."

"Of course it was. I was on the verge of busting a drug gang. I knew who the big men were at one end and the little men at the other. The only thing I didn't have was the connection. We had one of them in jail, a dealer called Sammy the Twig, but he wasn't talking. So it was arranged for me to be convicted and share a cell with him, to see if I could learn anything."

"So that was why you wanted me to leave you alone? And to think I felt sorry for you," she said bitterly.

"You nearly wrecked the whole thing." He sighed, then he added, "But I forgive you because you gave me a vital clue."

"*You* forgive *me*?" she echoed scathingly. "How kind of you! Should I be grateful—kneel and touch the floor with my forehead?"

"Considering what a mess you've made of a carefully planned operation, I think I've been very forbearing," he growled. "That refuge is being used as a clearing center for information and planning."

"What? I don't believe it."

"Of course. It's the perfect cover. There's no check on who uses it, so anyone can pass himself off as a tramp, stroll in, make his contact, and stroll out again. It's backed by the church and run by a load of innocent people who have no idea what's going on under their noses."

Diana sat down on the edge of the sofa as she realized that everything he said could be true.

"I'm sorry to give you a shock," Lee said more gently. "But with any luck we'll have them all mopped up soon, and the place will be clean again. Sammy the Twig saw that bit of paper you gave me. Fortunately the name persuaded him that I was one of them. After that he talked. He even gave me a message to take out for him. There's a big job coming up in the next few days, and all the plans are going through the refuge. There are several of us in there picking up what information we can. But now—" He ground his teeth.

"What about now?" Diana asked

"You've probably blown my cover."

"So I suppose I'm under suspicion as well? I'm probably one of them. When I gave you that address I was recruiting, wasn't I? And then I brought you away on purpose tonight because I was trying to spoil your operation.''

Lee stared at her in dismay, not because he believed a word of her self-accusation, but because it simply hadn't occurred to him. Though it should have. What had become of his instinctive suspicion, trained and honed by years in the force? She ought to have been the first person he suspected. Instead, their kiss had haunted him like the memory of honey and wine, dizzying his senses, undermining his detachment. "Don't talk nonsense!" he said roughly. "You're Judge Waldman's granddaughter.''

"So?" She shrugged. "I'm a rich, privileged bitch seeking a bit of illicit excitement.''

"Are you?"

"No, of course I'm not." She added, with a slight edge to her voice, "As you so rightly say, I'm Judge Waldman's granddaughter, and obviously a lot more innocent than I thought I was. I actually thought you needed my help, which is a laugh. Instead, you were cursing me for spoiling your bust. Well, you said it, didn't you? You said I was just playing Lady Bountiful.''

"I said a lot of things, I didn't mean that day, Diana. I also did something that I *did* mean. When this is over—hell! I have no right to think of anything right now except that my cover was probably blown when I came home with you.''

"No, it wasn't," Vita said from the door. "They'll just assume you're one of Diana's lame dogs.''

For the first time Lee realized that the other three had been standing in the hall, shamelessly eavesdropping through the half-open door. Diana didn't seem surprised.

Before he could respond the telephone rang. Diana answered it and almost immediately said, "Wait a moment. I'll take this in the study." She vanished next door.

"What do you mean, lame dogs?" Lee asked the others.

"Like us," Vita told him. "Di found us in the pound and brought us home."

"The pound?"

"Weren't you there tonight?"

"You mean the refuge?"

"That's right. Full of creatures that no one wants, all hoping someone will give them a home. We three got lucky. At least, Martin and I did. Clive will move on eventually."

"You mean—none of you are related to her at all?"

"I'm a student," Clive explained. "I got thrown out of my last place because I couldn't pay the rent. I went to the crypt every night to sleep. Di found me and offered me a room here. I pay for my food, but she won't take anything for the room."

"I used to be in an old folks' home," Vita said. "Dreadful. Like being stuck in a nursery again. I told this young nurse I wasn't going to take orders from her at my time of life even if she was wearing a uniform. She said the rules had to be respected, but you should have seen her face when I told her exactly what she could do with her rules." Vita cackled at the memory, and Lee found himself grinning. He instinctively warmed to the old woman who was bursting with life.

"I can't see you settling sedately into a home," he admitted.

"Course not!" Vita said with scorn. "I escaped."

"How did you manage on your own?"

"I had a wonderful time. But it couldn't last. They don't let you enjoy yourself, do they? Next thing I knew I was arrested for vagrancy by a young copper with his mother's milk still on him. I boxed his ears and ended up in court. Even the judge was young enough to be my son. He called me an elderly delinquent. I told him to mind his manners. He said he was sending me to jail to make sure I had a roof over my head. Blooming cheek!

"Jail was all right. But like the nursing home only the food was better. While I was in there, I heard about the refuge. I wasn't going back to that home. No fear. All those old dears watching the clock, hoping their kids would come to visit them, putting a brave face on when they didn't. It used to make me glad I didn't have any kids. Martin could tell you all about kids."

She finished with a knowing glance that made the old man bristle. "My son's okay," he said belligerently. "It's that woman he married. She was all over me at the start. I liked her, so I said they could live with me 'cause the house is big enough. Only then she starts trying to get me out, saying my mind's going. They actually asked the court to declare me incompetent. So I beat it out of there."

"And Diana found you at the refuge and brought you home?" Lee said, fascinated.

"She's always bringing people home for a couple of nights," Martin said.

"So no one will think anything of your leaving with her," Vita reassured him.

At that moment Diana returned. "Now, where were we?" she asked.

"We're just going to have supper," Vita said firmly. "And then you're going to bed, my girl. You've got a hard day tomorrow. Come on all of you." She indicted for Lee to come too.

"I must make a phone call first," Lee said.

He called the squad car that was parked two streets away from St. Mark's. "Any news from Grainger?" he demanded, naming the colleague who'd been working undercover with him in the crypt.

"Yes. He says it caused a bit of excitement when you left with that young woman, but our *friend* has been asking about her and apparently she's fond of down and outs. He seems to have written you off as just another sponger, so you'd better stay where you are for tonight. It would look odd if you came back. Where can we contact you?"

Lee gave them Diana's number, then hung up. Strangely, he felt very little sense of disappointment at being out of the action when it was heating up. The thought of staying here was pleasant.

Through the open door he could see Diana moving around in her study. She looked up when he knocked, her face expressing nothing but bland indifference. But he wasn't fooled. She was furious with him. "For the moment they want me to stay here and pose as one of your strays," he said. "Is that all right? I know it ruins your plans for throwing me out on my ear, but you can do that tomorrow."

"Far be it from me to interfere with a police operation," she said frostily. "Of course you can stay."

"Thank you," he said meekly. A glinting look from the most glorious pair of dark eyes he'd ever seen told him she'd seen through the meekness to the irony beneath. Pleasurable anticipation stirred in him at the thought of the battle to come.

"Are you two going to eat supper or would you prefer to starve?" Vita demanded from the doorway.

"We have a guest tonight, Vita," Diana said. "Mr—? I suppose I can know your name now?"

"Detective Inspector Lee Fortuno," he told her.

"The inspector will be staying the night."

"Or course he will. I've already made up his bed."

Suddenly Lee felt filthy. It had been three days since he'd washed or shaved. He also had an uncomfortable feeling that his clothes were alive. "I think I need a bath," he said uneasily.

"Eat first," Vita declared.

"I really don't think I should sit down in your clean kitchen like this."

"Come upstairs, I'll run you a bath," Vita offered.

He followed her up, and she showed him a bedroom with its own bathroom. The bed was made with spotless white linen. He looked at it longingly. "Is this where you defumigate everyone?" he asked.

"Them as wants it. Some prefer to live with the company they're used to, if you know what I mean." She went into the bathroom, started the water running, then returned with a large plastic bag. "Put your clothes in here, and I'll find something else for you to wear."

When she'd gone Lee stripped off thankfully. He was just heading for the bathroom when Vita's head appeared around the door. "Clive says—oh, sorry." She vanished again.

"It's all right," Lee called back with as much dignity as he could muster. "What does Clive say?"

"That you can borrow some of his things to wear," Vita shouted back through the door. She returned downstairs and found Diana waiting in the hall.

"What were you saying sorry for?" Diana queried.

"I walked in on him in the altogether. Don't look like that. I've seen more naked men than you've had hot breakfasts." She sighed nostalgically. "Ah, if only I were forty years younger. He's a well-made laddie."

"It's of no interest to me how well-made he is," Diana said stiffly.

Vita chuckled. "Liar," she said.

Three

I've put him in the book room," Vita said, returning to the kitchen. "Then he can have his supper in front of the fire. Poor soul, he looked as if he was half frozen as well as half starved."

"You're wasting your sympathy," Diana informed her crisply. "He's only pretending to be a tramp. He probably eats very well."

"Well, he doesn't *look* as if he did," Vita retorted unanswerably. She took Lee's supper out of the oven and departed. Diana heard murmurs of thanks as he received it. After a while Vita returned, saying, "He wanted to know if he'd been banished because you're cross with him, but I said you were sorry for the unkind things you said."

"I'm not sorry at all," Diana exclaimed, affronted. "And I shall tell him so."

"That's right, go and talk to him. You can take the wine with you."

"I shall do no such thing," Diana said, not at all pleased to find Lee being treated as an honored guest. "You're the one who wants to make a fuss over him. I think that glimpse of him you had must have addled your judgment." She caught Vita looking at her slyly and said, exasperated, "Oh, give him anything you like, although he probably prefers beer."

"No, I asked him about that. He likes wine, but he says any old red plonk will do."

Diana ground her teeth. "I don't keep any old red plonk in the house." She lifted a half-full bottle from the remains of the meal on the kitchen table. "This rather fine claret is all we have."

"I'll take him that, then," Vita said, whisking it from her hand and walking out, leaving Diana with a strange feeling of having been outwitted.

She lingered in the kitchen, unwilling to see Lee again. Her cheeks burned to think how she'd pitied his desolate state, and all the time he'd been cursing her as an interfering busybody. It was unlucky that he had to stay here tonight, but it should be possible to avoid him tomorrow morning. She began to compose a dignified good-night speech with polite regrets that they wouldn't be meeting the next day. When she was sure she had it perfect, she went to open the door of the book room. Then she stopped.

Lee was lying on the sofa with his eyes closed, his breathing regular. It would have been simple to leave him, but she couldn't resist the impulse to creep closer and see how different he looked after a bath and shave.

He was dressed in shirt and jeans, which, since Clive was half a size smaller, were too tight. He'd evidently abandoned the battle to keep the shirt buttons fixed, and now the edges lay open, revealing a smooth brown chest. The jeans seemed to have been wallpapered onto him. For their first meeting in the cell Diana had seen him in an old, baggy suit that concealed almost everything about his body. For sleeping in the refuge he'd added a raincoat shaped like a sack. But now there was nothing to hide the length of his legs, with their lean, taut thighs, or the narrowness of his hips.

His shirt sleeves were pushed back at the wrists, exposing muscular forearms and shapely, long-fingered hands, relaxed now, but full of latent power. She could still remember that power, how easily he'd held her. And the pressure of his body against hers had hinted at the unseen, tensile strength. The warning had been there if only she'd heeded it.

Letting her gaze travel upward, Diana saw the width of his shoulders, the smooth base of his throat, and the tousled hair. It had been dull before from rough living, but now he'd washed it and it gleamed blue-black in the lamplight. His face held her attention. Vita was right, she realized. He did look exhausted. There were dark smudges under his eyes, and he was sleeping in a concentrated way, like a man who knew he might not get the chance again for a while.

He'd shaved off the several days' growth of beard that had obscured the line of his jaw. Now she could see that it was clean-cut and decisive, with a touch of mulishness about the chin. His mouth was wide and as beautiful as she remembered. She should tear her eyes away from that mouth. It conjured up too many memories of how he'd pressed it against her lips, inflaming her as no man had ever done before. He'd kissed her only to be rid of her, yet she'd responded helplessly, like a green girl with her first embrace.

Now she understood the contradictory signals she'd received from him. Lee was no tramp, but a confident, handsome man, sure of himself and his place in the world.

Until their explosive meeting two months earlier, Diana had lived a life that was centered on her mind. Without conceit she knew that her memory was exceptional and her power to manipulate information and pursue more than one line of reasoning at the same time was a heaven-sent gift to a lawyer. She enjoyed her talent and the ability it gave her to help people.

She'd had infrequent romances with colleagues as brilliant and disciplined as herself, but she'd never been so deeply in love that it dominated her life. Both her emotions and her sensations were kept in proper order and the idea that they could get out of hand would have been foreign to her. Perhaps she had even been a little smug about that.

Then Lee had blasted the whole neat illusion apart with one shocking demonstration of erotic power. In a moment her world had turned upside down, revealing her to herself as a woman at the mercy of sensations so uncontrollable that they'd made her forget her surroundings, her responsibilities and her professional honor. She'd fled the man who'd made it happen like a refugee from a whirlwind.

In the weeks that followed she had gone through the whole gamut of emotions from scorn at herself to anger at Lee. But underneath every shifting mood had been the pulsating need to see him again.

Now he was here and there was nothing to stop her feasting her eyes on him, despite the inner voice that warned her if she wanted to retreat to her safe world she should back off now.

Cautiously she began to lean forward to retrieve his plate from the floor, moving quietly so as not to wake him.

"Diana..." He said her name so softly that she had to turn her head to see if she'd imagined it. He was lying with his eyes half open, watching her through the crack.

"I just came for your plate," she said, reaching for it. But somehow he'd sneaked an arm around her waist and was drawing her down to the sofa beside him.

"Are you still mad at me?" he asked sleepily.

"There wouldn't be a lot of point since you wouldn't take any notice. Will you please let me go?"

"But I'm comfortable like this," he objected.

Diana flattened her hands against his chest to prevent his drawing her any closer. His assurance was alarming. "You may be, but I'm not," she said.

"That's because you're sitting at an angle. If I move over you can get beside me."

She meant to argue, but somehow it seemed silly to make a fuss when there was so much room for both of them, and she found he was right. It was far more comfortable lying beside him. "Lee, we have to do some talking," she said.

"Of course we do. But we have important things to say to each other first," he said firmly, drawing her close.

She told herself that this time she was prepared for the devastating touch of his lips, but the reality made a mockery of her memories. Nothing that had happened since their first and last kiss had had any reality compared to the dazzling feelings that coursed through her as soon as his mouth touched hers. It was shameless to want to yield so completely, without even a pretense of resistance, but she discovered that she didn't mind being shameless. On the contrary, she rejoiced in it. It felt right for her body to be pressed intimately against his, so that she could make out every line of his hard, lean frame and sense the response to her that vibrated through him.

He was right in saying that they had things to communicate before they could talk. Now they were saying them, exchanging question and answer through the perfect communion of lips and tongues, through the warmth of their breath and the mingling heat of their bodies.

She felt her excitement rising to dangerous heights at the thought of the future, when she would know him more intimately. She was being carried into strange territory, and she had to put a brake on herself while there was still time. When she stiffened against him, she felt the effort at control in his tense muscles. Then he released her reluctantly, after which they lay looking at each other, each aware of the other's chest rising and falling and the soft thunder of their hearts. "I just wanted to be sure I hadn't imagined it," Lee said unsteadily.

She shook her head. "It was no illusion," she said.

"I thought about you all the time I was in jail, wishing we'd met some other way. I don't want you thinking of me as someone who needs a crutch."

"What does it matter how we met?"

"It might," he said cautiously. "But never mind that now. It's time we got properly introduced." Diana moved reluctantly away and he sat up, offering his hand. "How do you do."

"How do you do, Inspector," Diana said, shaking his hand.

"I wish you'd stop calling me 'Inspector' in that formal way," he complained.

"I'm trying to convince myself. I've met all kinds of policemen, but never one like you."

"I never did do things by the book," he agreed. "It's got me into a lot of trouble in the past. I'm wondering what kind of trouble I'm in this time."

"If you're afraid you can always back off," she offered, keeping firm hold of his hand.

"Nobody ever called Lee Fortuno a quitter," he said, twining his fingers with hers.

A coal fell in the gate, signaling to him that the fire was dying. "Let me make that up," he said. To get to it he had to step over the dog, who rolled onto his back, revealing himself as cross between a wolf hound and an elephant. "Good grief!" Lee said involuntarily.

Diana smiled. "It's all right. Fang's completely harmless."

"Fang?"

"I didn't choose his name," she said defensively. "His original owners gave it to him."

"How did he come to be yours?"

"I was driving home one day when I saw him sitting outside a house, crying to be let in. It was pouring with rain, and he looked so wretched that I went and knocked on the door. But one of the neighbors told me the people had moved several days ago. They just shut him out in the street and left him. The neighbor said his name was Fang, but she didn't know where the owners had gone." There was a thread of steel in her voice that startled him. "It's as well for them I never caught up with them."

"So you brought him home," Lee prompted.

"I had to. He was drenched and hungry. I meant to find a home for him but no one wants a dog that size."

"I wonder why," Lee murmured satirically.

"Gradually he just became one of the family."

"Well, he must be a handy guard dog," Lee suggested, venturing to give Fang a tentative pat.

"Oh, no, he's utterly useless," Diana said with a chuckle. "One day Vita locked him out of the house by mistake when she went shopping. There was no one else in, so he simply flung his weight against the French windows until they opened. She came home to find them standing wide, and Fang asleep on my bed. Anyone could have got in for all he cared."

"And this one?" Lee asked, tickling the cat who was nuzzling him.

"Suki just wandered in and adopted us." She saw his expression and laughed. "There's a goldfish, too."

"I'm quite prepared to hear that the goldfish wandered in," Lee said faintly. "He was probably wearing a top hat and tails and doing a soft-shoe shuffle."

"That's just ridiculous," Diana said severely. "His name is John Wayne. Whenever did you ever hear of John Wayne in top hat and tails?"

"Now I come to think of it, I didn't," he agreed, eyeing her, fascinated. "Diana, I know I'm going to regret asking this, but how do you come to have a goldfish called John Wayne?"

"He belonged to my neighbors. They asked me to take him when they went abroad. I did, and it was a great mistake. For one thing he's temperamental and for another it's a constant struggle to stop Suki having him for lunch."

"A goldfish—temperamental?" Lee queried, ready to believe anything.

"Oh, yes. He has a filthy temper. He sulks for hours, and we all go in fear and trembling. I don't know why I agreed to have him."

"You agreed because you couldn't do anything else, you crazy lady," Lee observed tenderly. "Tell me, Diana, have you ever turned your back on a stray?"

"Why should I?" she asked, puzzled. "I've got plenty of room."

"Yes, but—" He checked himself, deciding it would be wiser to leave it there for now. They had a tricky road to negotiate together. On one level they already knew each other intimately, but they still had to discover how well they related when out of the magic circle of each other's arms. Just now he didn't want to worry about the fact that this strongly protective woman had first been drawn to him as a lame dog when the truth about him was very different. All he wanted was to watch her sitting on the floor sipping wine, her rich beauty glowing in the firelight.

"I suppose you think this household is pretty strange?" she said.

"Only at first glance. In some ways it reminds me of my own home. I'm Italian by birth. My parents moved here when I was ten. My aunt had married an Englishman, and she loved England so they decided to give it a try. At first they lived with her family. Even when they had their own home there was always some uncle or aunt or grandparent visiting us from the old country.''

''Tell me about it,'' she said in a voice whose wistfulness struck a poignant note in his heart. ''Who is there in your family?''

''There's Mama and Papa, me, my two younger sisters, Maria and Antonia, and Carlo, my brother, who's only fifteen.''

''You're the firstborn, then?'' Diana interrupted him.

''Yes.''

''I expect that made it easier for your sisters.''

''You mean the old idea about Italians preferring sons? Perhaps some of them do, but my parents didn't care one way or the other. Girls, boys, we were all loved and welcomed. If they had a favorite at all I think it's Maria.'' Lee's face softened. ''Maria is just a year younger than me, and when we were children we were always in mischief together. She used to take the blame for my misdeeds, because Papa couldn't bear to be angry with her.''

''You *let* her take the blame?'' Diana queried.

Lee grinned. ''Of course I did. I'm not a fool. My cunning little sister doesn't do anything for nothing. I paid my debts by doing her homework, and then again when she started going out with boys. My parents made me go along too, to keep an eye on them. But as soon as we were out of sight we went our separate ways, meeting up again when it was time to go home.''

Diana watched him, enchanted by these tales and the effect they had on Lee. He'd been granted the most priceless gift of all, a happy childhood, and now the memory of it seemed to glow forth from him. She watched him closely as he went on, ''I can't recall either of my parents being angry for long. We were too much a united family for that. Everyone laughed and squabbled together, and seemed to live each moment at the tops of their voices. There were no secrets in our house.

"The first time I fell in love I was about seventeen. I was so terribly serious and self-conscious about it. Antonia and Maria teased me mercilessly, so I put on a big act of not really caring about this girl. Then when I finally took her home, Antonia greeted her with the words 'Are you the girl my brother says can jump in the river for all he cares?'"

Diana rocked with laughter. Some of Lee's own warmth seemed to reach out and envelop her, conjuring up the scene before her eyes. It was a delightful scene, set in a golden aureole, filled with people who could risk teasing because they trusted the bonds of blood and affection that united them. "I expect you spend a lot of time with them," she said wistfully.

"Not as much as I'd like. Mama and Papa got homesick for the old country about ten years ago, so they went back. I was twenty-two and just getting settled in my job, so I stayed here. Maria stayed with me for a while, but then she went to Italy for a holiday and my cunning parents arranged for her to meet lots of good-looking Italian boys." Lee shrugged. "Next thing, Maria calls me to say 'Come to my wedding.' So now I'm alone."

Looking at his handsome face in the flickering firelight, Diana wondered just how alone he was. "You must miss them a lot," she said.

"All the time. That whole wonderful way of life is a legacy that stays with you forever. It's hard to settle for anything else."

"Yes, it must be," she murmured, staring abstractedly into the fire.

"What about you, Diana? Do you have brothers or sisters?"

She was silent so long that he thought she wasn't going to answer. But then, still without looking at him, she said, "My life's been quite different than yours. You know my grandfather was Judge Waldman. I went to live with him when I was ten years old."

"Just the two of you?"

"Just the two of us."

Lee whistled. "That couldn't have been a bundle of laughs."

Diana smiled wryly. "He was totally honorable, scrupulous and upright. He paid his debts to the last penny, and justice was his god. But he certainly wasn't a bundle of laughs."

"You poor kid. I saw him in action a few times at the end of his career. He was terrifying."

"Don't feel too sorry for me," Diana said quickly. "He was a kind man, and he did his best for me. He didn't know how to talk to children so he addressed me like an adult, and I certainly preferred that to being talked down to. When I became interested in the law, we started to get on really well."

Diana didn't say that she'd come to understand that her grandfather loved her by a process of logical reasoning rather than through any demonstration of affection. Judge Waldman approved of logic. It was what he understood best, and the granddaughter he'd cared for so scrupulously had only divined the truth at the very end. But although words flowed from her golden tongue in court, she wouldn't have known how to express something so close to her heart.

"How did you come to be living with him?" Lee asked. "Did your parents die?"

For a moment Diana hovered on the brink of telling him everything, including the painful secret that she'd never entrusted to another living soul. This vibrant, spontaneous man was like a magnet, drawing her toward him with tantalizing hints of a magic world to be discovered in his company. Surely, just this once, she could dare to open her heart? But a lifetime of controlling her responses couldn't be ignored, and the impulse withered. "That's right," she said briefly. Before he could ask any more questions she went on "He left me this house. It's where we lived together."

"I wondered how such a modern woman came to be in this Victoria pile," he observed.

"It's a beautiful house," she flared.

"Sure it is," he said soothingly. "I love it. It's got character. But it's huge. It must have looked pretty gloomy to a child, and it would be even gloomier now if you had to live in it alone. I can understand that you want to fill it with people."

He hoped this might provoke Diana into revelations about her sympathy for waifs and strays, so that he might start to discover the key to her nature. But instead of rising to the bait she began to tell him about the house's history. To a man brought up in a home where everyone spoke their thoughts as soon as they thought them, Diana's reticence was tantalizing. He'd held her in his arms and knew that shoals of passion whirled beneath her cool exterior. When she laughed the sound was vibrant, hinting at rich veins of feeling waiting to be tapped. Yet he was always aware of a mysterious, invisible barrier, as though they were talking through glass.

As she reached out to pour him some more claret, the movement revealed her slim forearm with a cheap plastic watch around the wrist. Lee studied it, fascinated by its tackiness against her elegance, for even in chunky sweater and jeans Diana looked like a thoroughbred. "You were wearing a delicate little gold watch when we first met," he recalled. "This one must have cost you about fifty pence."

She shook her head, her eyes dancing with mischief. "Forty pence," she said. "I get a discount for bulk."

"You buy these in bulk?"

She reached past him to a low shelf and pulled out a cardboard box that contained about forty similar watches. "I buy them from a market stall, four dozen at a time," she told him.

"But why?"

"Because they get stolen at the refuge. This one—" she waved her wrist "—would have been stolen tonight if I hadn't left so soon."

"You don't mind them stealing from you? I mean, isn't that a little ungrateful when you're trying to help them?"

"Why should they feel grateful to me?" she demanded with a passionate intensity that took him by surprise. "What have they got in their lives that I or anyone else should feel entitled to gratitude? Stealing my watch is the most fun they ever get."

"But what do they do with them? I can't believe there's much of a black market in plastic watches."

"They don't want to sell them. They prize them as symbols that just for once they won. They beat the system and got away with it."

She was magical, he thought, with her eyes shining with enthusiasm for her protégés. But a policeman's natural suspicion forced him to say, "Diana, doesn't it occur to you that your passion for lame dogs leaves you open to every kind of con man?"

"Of course it does. Don't forget I'm a lawyer. I've met as many bad characters as you have, and I can tell when someone isn't what they seem."

"Can you indeed?" he queried satirically, raising one eyebrow. "I don't recall that this percipience was a notable feature of our first meeting."

"Very funny!" she said, reddening slightly. "That was entirely different. I can spot a crook trying to fool me that he's respectable, but not many people are crazy enough to pretend to be crooks if they don't have to. Anyway, you didn't deceive me entirely. You were like no tramp I'd ever met before. That was what confused me."

"Yes, we both knew there was something unusual going on, didn't we?" he said thoughtfully. "You weren't the only one who was confused. When I first saw you, dressed austerely for court, I thought you were like the embodiment of your name, 'Diana, the chaste moon goddess.' But then I held you in my arms, and I realized that the moon goddess was only half the story. Underneath there's a woman who's haunted me night and day. There's very little do to in prison except brood. You were always there, making me wonder until I nearly went crazy wondering. If we hadn't met by chance tonight, I was going to come and find you."

"I wonder what you would have said to me," she mused.

"The same thing I'd like to say to you now. Let's forget the circumstances of our first meeting and begin again, seeing each other clearly this time."

"You'd *like* to say?" she queried.

"Right this minute I can't concentrate on anything but this job I'm working on. But when it's over—which will be soon—I'm going to come back, Diana. And the next time we meet, it will be *me* that you see."

Four

––––––

Diana came downstairs to find Lee already dressed and sitting at the kitchen table while Vita urged food into him. "How can I look like a convincing tramp if you fatten me up?" he grumbled.

"Have another egg," Vita said, depositing one on his plate. Lee made a play of groaning, but he ate the egg. Vita was an excellent cook.

"Are you still going to be under cover?" Diana asked, sitting opposite him.

"Until the job's finished, but that won't be long. I'm hoping to wrap it up tonight."

"Does it mean trouble at the refuge?" she asked worriedly.

Lee shook his head. "The deals have all been finalized and the action will move somewhere else. But I won't want you to go there until I contact you and tell you it's all right."

"Oh really?" she said, nettled by his self-assured tone. "I'm sorry, but I can't oblige. Surely you realize I've got to warn Gavin what's happening?"

"I'll do that. It's important that he carries on as normal. I want you to stay away in case anyone's watching for you. Now I've got to go."

She'd have liked to argue about his high-handed way of giving her orders, but the thought of his going drove everything else out of her mind. "I'll drive you into town," she said quickly.

"No, I don't want to be seen with you again. I'll take a bus—" he assumed an excruciating accent "—if yer could spare the bus fare for a poor feller as is dahn on 'is luck, bless yer lidy."

"How can you make jokes when it's all so serious?" she demanded tensely.

Lee shrugged. "It's because it's all so serious that I survive by making jokes," he said lightly. "That's true of a lot of the police. You should get to know us some time instead of instinctively siding against us and accusing us of harassment at the drop of a hat." When she looked startled he added softly, "A passion for the underdog can ruin your sense of proportion."

Clive appeared in the kitchen door. "I'm on my way to college," he said to Lee. "I can run you into town. My car's as battered as you are, so it won't rouse suspicion."

"Thanks," Lee said.

He went into the hall, and Diana followed him. "I'll be in touch soon," he promised. "Next time we meet I want to be able to give you all my attention."

"I thought I had it last night," she murmured.

He shook his head, his eyes mischievous. "You wait until I've got nothing else on my mind. Then you'll see." The laughter drained from his face. "We have a lot of unfinished business."

He kissed her. It wasn't a kiss of passion, but of reassurance and promise for the future. Then he walked out and squeezed into Clive's old clunker. Diana watched him, still conscious of the imprint of his mouth on hers. She closed the door, suddenly feeling dreadfully bereft.

She had a successful morning, persuading an opponent to settle out of court in the last moments before the trial was due to begin, thus avoiding having to reveal that her client's chief witness had fled the country that morning. But it meant she had an unexpectedly free afternoon and too much time to brood.

She told herself that what was happening was impossible. She didn't believe in love at first sight. Real love, the kind that led to marriage, built its foundations on sympathies of mind as well as heart, on liking and respect, and steady affection that would endure for years. This riotous, unruly upsurge of feeling was no more than a mood that would run its course and die. But instead of being relieved at the thought, she knew a swell of near panic that the anguished joy possessing her might end. She wanted it to last forever and bring her sweet fulfillment. And if instead it brought her only pain, she would accept that too, as long as she could experience every feeling through to the end.

There was no call from Lee that evening, but she hadn't really expected it. Tomorrow was the soonest she could hope to hear from him.

She was awakened early the next morning by Vita shaking her urgently, exclaiming, "He did it!"

Diana sat up in bed to find Vita had switched on the little television she kept in the bedroom. And there was Lee, looking tired but pleased, talking to someone about the arrest he'd made in the early hours of the morning. Through the last haze of sleep she heard the interviewer saying, "months of painstaking work... triumphant conclusion... drug ring behind bars for a long time..."

All through breakfast Diana was listening for the phone to ring. But when it did it was for Clive. The sharp stab of disappointment made her clench her hands under the table. This was foolishness, she told herself. Lee had a lot of paperwork to do. He'd call her as soon as he could.

She had a busy day in court. When she returned to her desk late afternoon, there was a sheaf of messages waiting for her, but nothing from Lee. She called to tell Vita she'd be home early, and after a few minutes of meaningless conversation hung up without having sunk her pride enough to ask if he'd called the house. She would have been dismayed if she could have seen Vita replace the receiver, turn to Martin and say, "She's got it bad."

And Martin's reply: "About time too. I was beginning to worry about her."

"You!" Vita sniffed contemptuously. "I was worrying about her before you ever showed your face here."

Diana arrived home to find her favorite meal on the table, cooked to perfection. Afterward she retired to her study to read over her notes for the following day's case, which she already knew perfectly. At ten o'clock Vita brought her some tea and a slice of cake. "Martin's started getting his gardening tools ready for spring," she said.

"It's a little soon for that, isn't it?" Diana said mechanically.

"He thinks the weather will improve at any moment. He's full of plans for what he's going to do this year."

"That's fine."

"Well, I'll be off now. I won't disturb you any longer. You'll call me if you want some more tea?"

Diana smiled. "I can get it myself, Vita."

"Don't you stir. I can do it. Eat up that cake. I made it specially. And stop worrying."

"I'm not worried," Diana said coolly. She indicated her notes. "I have a very strong case."

Vita, who hadn't been talking about tomorrow's case, went quietly away.

Diana stayed at her desk until one in the morning. Then she went to bed. The phone hadn't rung.

Only the discipline of a lifetime kept her going the next day. She spent the evening in the same way as the night before, and still there was no call from Lee. On the third evening, unable to bear the sympathetic looks and hushed tones of the others a moment longer, she put on her old clothes and headed for the refuge. If there had ever been any danger to her, it was surely over now.

She was about halfway there when she realized that the same pair of headlights had been in her rearview mirror for ages. She went faster, and the car behind her did the same. She took a sudden turn and after a moment the other car appeared behind her again.

Coincidence, she told herself. But when she slowed, the car also slowed, refusing to pass her. She peered into the mirror but it was dark, and the dazzling light from the following headlights obliterated her pursuer's details. Someone was very determinedly sticking to her, refusing to be thrown off.

How could this be happening when Lee had pulled the gang in? Unless some of them had got away? It would take her another ten minutes to reach her destination, and the streets didn't become lonely until the last moment. She should be safe enough. But there was something about being followed that made the hair stand up on the back of her neck.

She accelerated the last half mile, reaching the church well ahead of her pursuer. She jumped out and hurried down the steps to the crypt. Just then, Gavin appeared at the entrance and she signaled to him. "Are you all right?" he asked, coming up to her.

"There's someone following me," she said softly. "Did you get a call from Detective Inspector Fortuno?"

"Yes. I was appalled. But it explains some of the newcomers we've been having recently."

"Has anything happened here?"

"Not a thing, except that the new faces have disappeared. I gather he made some arrests. But what's this about your being followed? You don't mean—?"

"I don't know. Lee said it might happen, but I didn't believe him. It seems he was right. Whoever it is should be here about now."

"We can get him as he comes down the stairs," Gavin said.

Above them they heard a car stop, then someone get out and started descending the stairs. They watched as a pair of long, masculine legs came into view. Diana, standing farther back than Gavin, couldn't see the man's face in the dim light, but she held herself tensed, ready to help bring their quarry down.

The scuffle was a short one. Gavin pounced. The intruder fought back, and Gavin ended the matter with a thundering left hook that sent him to the ground. After regaining some composure, he seemed to remember that he was a man of the cloth and looked self-conscious. "It's nice to know I can still throw a good punch in the cause of righteousness," he said. "Let's have a look at him, then I'll call the police."

He leaned over the young man who was sitting under the lamp and rubbing his jaw. Diana came to stand beside him. Then she stiffened with horror. "Oh no!" she groaned.

"You know him?" Gavin asked.

"It's Clive. He's staying in my house. Clive!" She knelt beside him.

Clive looked at her, exasperated. "Thanks a lot!" he said. "That's the last time I try to do you a favor."

"I take it that I haven't apprehended a criminal," Gavin said, sounding disappointed. He helped Diana assist Clive to his feet and together they took him into the kitchen. "My apologies," he said, pouring Clive a strong cup of tea.

"Don't worry," Clive said darkly, glaring at Diana. "I know who to blame. That was a terrific punch, though."

"I boxed at university," Gavin explained proudly.

"Really? So do I—"

"You don't mind if I interrupt these pugilistic reminiscences, I hope?" Diana said coldly. "Clive, what on earth were you doing creeping about after me in that suspicious manner?"

"I was keeping a protective eye on you, as I promised Lee I would. And that's all the thanks I get."

Gavin tactfully made himself scarce. Diana hardly noticed. She was preoccupied with something Clive had said. "You promised Lee?" she echoed incredulously. "You mean he asked you to protect me?"

"Not exactly protect," Clive said with a cautious look at her infuriated expression. "Just keep an eye on you. He was pretty sure you'd do something rash."

"He actually *said* that?"

"Yes. He said you had a bossy nature and were so used to giving orders that you probably weren't much good at taking them, and he wanted me to watch you as unobtrusively as possible because there was no point in making you mad and unreasonable. He's got a point, Di. I mean," Clive added hastily as he saw her face, "about your being used to giving orders."

The fact that this was true didn't make her feel better. "You should have told him to mind his own business."

"I thought this *was* his business," Clive said mildly. "He's the police officer in charge, after all."

"He's not in charge of *me*, whatever he thinks," Diana said, seething.

"Look, it's not a crime for him to be concerned for you." He put a placating hand on her arm. "I'm sorry I gave you a fright, Di, but don't get worked up about this. After all, I was the one who ended up with the black eye."

"You'd better let me drive you home," she said stiffly.

"I'll get myself home in my own car, thank you," Clive said with dignity.

Without another word Diana turned and left. She hurried to her car and got in, slamming the door. She was bewildered and dismayed by the storm of feeling that buffeted her. How *dared* Lee do this!

It wasn't his attempt to protect her that made her recoil. Later she might even be able to see the funny side of that. What she couldn't cope with was the disturbing accuracy with which he'd penetrated her mind. It was as though he'd reached into it, brushing clumsy fingers against the sensitive filaments, and they'd flinched, curling it on themselves, rejecting his intrusion but unable to prevent it.

As long as she could remember, Diana had guarded the privacy of her mind. When she was very young, her warring parents had each tried to use her as a pawn. She'd learned to watch her tongue because the most innocent remark would be seized on, inflated and subtly altered to prove that she was an ally.

By the time she was ten the grave little girl had learned her first lesson about life: someone who knew what you were thinking could manipulate you. After that, she made certain no-one was privy to what she was thinking unless she wanted it known.

Now Lee Fortuno had invaded her mind, brushing aside barriers she had thought impregnable, and had had the nerve to size her up.

She drove around for an hour until she'd cooled down, then returned home. Clive was already there, and from the silence that fell as she appeared she guessed they'd all been talking about her. She was galled by the pity she was sure she could see in their eyes, but she managed to smile and bid them goodnight.

Clive caught up with her as she mounted the stairs. "I'm sorry I offended you," he said.

"You don't have to apologize," she told him lightly. "Are you afraid I'll throw you out of the house?"

"No, you'd never stoop so low. I just don't like to see you unhappy."

"I'm not unhappy. Don't be absurd."

"Aren't you? I know you were expecting Lee to come back, and I'm sure he will, Di, if only you're patient—"

She silenced him with a smile that was like a glass wall. "My dear boy, you mustn't be so melodramatic. What possible difference can it make whether he comes back or not?" She laughed. "Were you picturing me as 'patience on a monument, smiling at grief'? You should know me better by now."

She ran on up the stairs and escaped into her room. But somehow Lee seemed to slip inside with her, laughing as he recalled himself at seventeen, saying, "She can jump in the river for all I care," to hide the desperate vulnerability of love.

Of all the people in the world Lee would best understand the pain in her heart now, a pain that no amount of reasoning could ease. She sat on her bed in the darkness, wrapping her arms around herself as a defense against a terrible feeling of loneliness. But the only person who could defend her against it wasn't here.

Hugh called her the next morning to remind her that she'd promised to have dinner at his home that evening. "Mother's looking forward so much to seeing you," he said.

It had gone out of her head, yet she didn't feel able to cancel now and disappoint Leila Marriott. Besides, she refused to sit at home moping. "I'm looking forward to seeing her too," she said decisively.

She went, and heeded all her strength of mind to endure the evening. Hugh had rented a villa on Lake Como for a month in the summer so that his mother could enjoy the Italian sun. The two of them were determined to persuade her to join them. "Don't worry, Nigel won't be there," Hugh promised.

"Darling," Leila said, half laughing, half reproving.

"Face facts, Mother. If we're going to persuade Diana to become a part of this family, it may be necessary to disown my younger brother," Hugh joked.

"Ignore him, Leila," Diana said, quickly turning aside from the idea of marriage. "Nigel's all right. He just needs to grow up a little."

"But you'll come to Lake Como, won't you?" Hugh said.

"Don't think you'll be burdened with an invalid," Leila put in quickly. "My nurse will care for me. I shan't play gooseberry," she added significantly.

They wanted her so much, and it felt good to be wanted. Besides, the prospect of spending a month at an Italian lake with a man who adored her was enticing. And yet . . .

"Let me think about it," she hedged. "I will if I can shift my work load."

"I'll try to be patient," Hugh said, disappointed. "But you will come to that charity dinner with me, won't you?"

"Charity dinner?"

"Darling, I get the strangest feeling that you're not with us tonight. I spent half an hour telling you about that dinner just before we sat down."

"Yes, of course I remember," she said quickly. "I'd love to come."

It was four days since Lee had gone away, then five, then six. A week had passed, and she had to face facts. The torrent of emotions that had swept her up had meant nothing to him. He'd simply been enjoying a pleasant evening. All the discipline that had served her so well at other times was called into action now. After all, it was simply a matter of filing the experience under lessons of life and putting it aside.

Yet pain and disillusion refused to be ignored so easily, and they made her nights sleepless, casting a gray pall over her days. They also made her nervy and unpredictable.

"I should creep about on tiptoe if I were you," Vita muttered to Clive when he came in one Saturday afternoon. "She's in that terribly cheerful mood that means she's breaking up inside."

"Let's see what sort of a mood she's in when she hears what I have to say," Clive observed.

"Be careful you don't end up with another black eye," Martin warned.

Clive went and stood in the door of Diana's study. She glanced up and said briefly, "Is it important, Clive?"

"It depends how much you want to know what happened to Lee."

"I thought that subject was in the past. You're determined to make a romantic tragedy out of it, aren't you?"

"As a matter of fact, it nearly was a tragedy. All the time you've been cursing him up hill and down dale, he's been lying at death's door. Still, if you're not interested..."

He began to withdraw, but Diana was out of her chair and across the room in a flash. Her face was very pale. "What do you mean, death's door?" she demanded. "Clive, is this one of your jokes?"

"I don't call getting shot in the chest a joke."

"But—he was all right," she said wildly. "I saw him on the early news..."

"This was immediately afterward. One of the prisoners managed to fight his way free in the station and get to a gun. They caught him again, but not before Lee had stopped a bullet." He saw her deathly face and ventured to touch her arm. "It's all right, Di," he said gently. "He's out of danger now."

"Where is he?"

"St. Swithin's Hospital."

Diana was out into the hall before he'd finished speaking, pulling on her coat. Clive followed her to the front door, but before leaving she stopped and said, "Clive how did you discover all this?"

"I called the police station and asked to speak to him—which is what *you* should have done."

She hurried out to her car without answering, but his words haunted her on the journey. It was pride that had stopped her making the first move to contact Lee, and he might have died without her ever knowing.

It took half an hour to get to the hospital. She parked the car, then hurried in to find reception. "Where can I find Detective Inspector Fortuno?" she asked.

The middle-aged woman on the desk frowned. "Are you a relative?"

"I'm an attorney," Diana replied with as much professional dignity as she could muster. When the receptionist still looked doubtful, she crossed her fingers and added shamelessly, "I understand from the message that he wanted to see me without delay."

"Well, he shouldn't really—but if it's a police matter—room 15 on the second floor."

"Thank you." Diana hurried away before anyone else tried to detain her.

Her throat was strangely dry as she reached the second floor. She wasn't often troubled by self-doubt, but suddenly all her confidence drained away. Suppose he really didn't want to see her? After all, he *could* have sent her a message, and he hadn't. But she couldn't endure another moment without seeing Lee, touching him and reassuring herself that he was still there, rediscovering the warm smile that started far back in his dark eyes. She paused outside his door, took a deep breath, and entered.

She had a confused impression that there were several people in the room, but they were a blur. The only thing that was clear was the sight of Lee propped up against a mass of pillows, his face pale and drawn but lighting up with joy at the sight of her. He opened his arms and she went into them.

Five

─────

For a long moment Diana's lips lay against Lee's in the most fulfilling and yet most frustrating kiss she had ever known: fulfilling because she was where her heart told her she belonged, and frustrating because she didn't dare embrace him strongly. That must wait. For the moment she could only hold him gently, and sense with dismay how thin illness had made him. "My darling," she whispered when she could speak, "if only I'd known. How bad is it?"

"It's a lot better now," he murmured, his eyes twinkling.

"I never dreamed there was anything wrong with you. When I saw you on the news, you were all right . . ." The words ended in a choke.

"You're crying," he said tenderly.

"I'm not," she said at once.

"All right, you're not. Here, take my hanky."

"Well, you're enough to make a saint weep," she declared, drying her cheeks. "How bad is it? You look awful." Now that the first euphoria had passed, she saw his pallor and sunken eyes.

"The worst is over, I promise. Don't worry, darling. I'm a lot tougher than I look."

Diana became aware that they weren't alone. Turning, she saw three other people in the room. A man and woman in their sixties stood watching with pleased smiles on their faces. The man was an older version of Lee, tall and still lean, with an expressive, swarthy face, which must have been handsome in his youth. The woman was short and plump, with white hair and shrewd eyes that were taking in every detail of Diana.

"These are my parents," Lee said. "They came over from Italy to be with me. Mama, Papa, this is Diana."

A quick glance of suppressed amusement passed between the couple. Papa shook Diana's hand, but Mama studied her and said, "Diana? Your name is *Diana*?"

"That's right," she confirmed, puzzled by the intense scrutiny.

"I've wanted to meet you, Diana," Mama said. "My son has talked of you—not that we could make out too many words, but the tone was clear enough."

A crack of laughter came from a woman near the window. She was in her thirties, a handsome solid matron with black hair. "Look at him," she crowed, pointing at Lee who was gazing frantically around for a place to hide. "He's blushing. And well you might blush, brother dear, after the things we've been hearing."

"Allow me to introduce my sister, Maria," Lee said with what little dignity he could muster. "Not that I'm anxious to claim her, you understand, but I've been stuck with her for years.''

Diana shook hands with Maria, whom she instinctively liked. ''What have you been hearing?'' she asked.

''Nothing,'' Lee growled. ''I may have mentioned you once or twice, that's all.''

''You keep quiet,'' Maria ordered him. ''You don't know anything about it.'' Like her brother she looked Italian and had been born in that country, but years of growing up in England had taught them both to speak the language naturally. Their parents, on the other hand, still spoke with the strong accents of born and bred Italians. ''He's been unconscious, you see,'' Maria said to Diana, ''and he mumbled all the time about someone called Diana. We've been longing to meet you and see if all the things he said were true.''

''I want a cup of coffee,'' Mama declared, taking pity on her son, who looked as if he would like to vanish beneath the bedclothes. ''We go to the canteen, *all* of us,'' she added, firmly taking Maria's arm. ''We return later.''

''Thank you, Mama,'' Lee said faintly.

The three of them made their farewells and slipped out, leaving Diana and Lee alone. He opened his arms again. ''We may not have long,'' he said. ''Let's not waste it.''

She kissed him with aching tenderness. Despite his weakness Lee embraced her purposefully, his lips full of passionate intent. ''I dreamed every day that you came,'' he whispered.

''Why didn't you get someone to call me?'' she demanded urgently.

"Because the doctors have been pumping me full of drugs, and I've been woozy. My dreams have been full of Diana, but I couldn't remember your last name. I still can't."

"Waldman," she said, pressing him gently back against the pillows. He lay there tiredly, keeping hold of her hand.

"Ah yes, Waldman. Any relation to Lord Justice Waldman?"

"I'm his granddaughter," she said, dismayed.

"So you are. I expect you told me. Don't look so horrified, darling. It's only the drugs. My memory exists in patches. I know I'm in love with you, but I can't remember how we met. I don't know how long we've known each other, only that we're going to know each other all our lives. If only—" He wrinkled his brows. "There's something about you that has me worried. You don't happen to know what it is, do you?"

"You didn't mention it."

"Never mind. It can't matter all that much." He reached up and touched her face gently. "So you're the Diana who's haunted my dreams. I was afraid to wake and find you didn't really exist."

"And all this time I've been afraid that I'd dreamed what happened between us," she said huskily.

"Tell me what happened. I think I'll enjoy hearing."

"We met in a police cell. I thought you'd been arrested, but actually you were under cover. You did everything you could to get rid of me, including—"

"I remember that bit," he said contentedly. "The important parts of our acquaintance stand out in my mind. It's just the spaces in between that are vague. What happened then?''

"You went to jail and we met again two months later, in the refuge where I sometimes work. You were still under cover."

"Ah yes, it's coming back. Someone made a lunge for you and I broke my cover to defend you, which no good policeman would do. My chief read the riot act to me about that. You see what a bad effect you have on me? And then you kidnapped me. After that it's vague except that you kissed me and you have a gold-fish called John Wayne." He wrinkled his brow again. "Or perhaps I'm called John Wayne and you kissed the goldfish."

"That's enough for now," she said quickly, seeing how weary he looked. "I'm going to go away and come back when you're less tired."

To her relief a nurse came in at that moment. "I think you should get some rest now, Inspector," she said. "You really shouldn't be discussing police business for a while."

"Police—?"

"I explained at reception that I was an attorney," Diana interrupted hastily, "and about the message you left on my answering machine asking me to come here."

Lee's eyes gleamed with mischief. "Ah yes, another of the things I'd forgotten. Go away, lawyer. I'm not strong enough yet for what you do to me."

His parents and sister came in to say their fare-wells. Diana slipped out into the corridor, feeling shaken. His pallor and air of frailty had torn at her heart. The wave of fierce, protective love that had swept over her had almost made her break down. She had mastered the impulse, but it shocked her to realize how often, in Lee's company, the control she had perfected over years threatened to give way.

She could hear noises coming from behind the door. Lee's family was preparing to come out. Part of her wanted to stay and talk to them but part of her couldn't face anyone while she was in this nervous state. As she saw the door beginning to open she fled.

It was a couple of hours before she felt ready to go home and face the curious expressions she knew would greet her. She arrived to find everyone in the kitchen. Martin was going through a gardening catalog, Vita was making pastry, and Clive had his head buried in his books. As she entered they glanced up with ostentatious casualness, and Diana waited for the first curious question. But Vita said, "Hugh called you five times this evening. Something about a charity dinner you were supposed to be going to tonight."

"Oh ye gods," Diana whispered, coming down to earth with a bump. "I forgot all about it. What did you tell him?"

"Only that you were called away suddenly," Clive said. "Vita was exquisitely tactful. He wanted you to call him back as soon as you got in."

Guiltily Diana called Hugh. She didn't feel up to telling him the truth, so she invented a client with a desperate emergency, but in the end she knew that Hugh didn't believe her. Nevertheless, he received her apologies more in sorrow than in anger, merely commenting, "I don't know what's come over you these days Diana. You *never* forget things, even in an emergency."

"I know, but this time I did," she said humbly. "I'm sorry, Hugh."

She hung up and turned to find the others gathered around looking at her, but nobody said a word. The silence was deafening.

"I've been to see Lee," she said. "He was badly hurt, but he's going to be all right. Honestly I don't know what you were all worried about."

The next day she arrived at the hospital before the family. She was relieved to see Lee looking stronger and more alert. His voice was stronger, too. "I've sorted out my memories now," he said. "*You're* John Wayne and *I* kissed the goldfish."

"Fool," she said tenderly, and showed her delight in a lingering kiss.

"Well, anyway, I've remembered everything," he said after a while, "including why I'm never going to let you get away from me."

"That's very satisfactory," she said lightly. "Have you also remembered what it is about me that worries you?"

There was the merest fraction of a second's pause before he said, "Did I say that? My mind must have been wandering."

"Perhaps you were confusing me with some other woman," she teased.

"That's always possible," he said with aplomb. "And whatever made you think I was going to fall into that trap, Madam Attorney?"

"It was worth a try."

"You're dealing with a policeman. I've been cross-examined by enough clever lawyers to be able to cope with anything you can throw at me."

"You wait. I'll think of something."

They drew apart self-consciously as the door opened and the family entered. Diana could see at once that something was wrong. Despite her bright, determined smile Mama looked as if she had been crying. Maria was also smiling, but in her case it masked a fierce anger. Papa hovered protectively over his wife.

When the first greeting had been exchanged, Lee looked closely at his mother and said, "Mama, what's the matter?"

"Niente," she said firmly. "Now you are getting better there is nothing the matter."

"Are you sure you haven't been crying?"

"Of course not. But I sleep badly. London is so different from our little village."

Lee let the subject drop, although Diana was sure he wasn't fooled. She went out into the corridor to let his family have him to themselves, and as she had hoped Maria followed her out a moment later. "What's happened?" she asked.

"Our money has been stolen," Maria said in a low voice.

"When did this happen?"

"Mama found the money missing this morning when she looked for it to pay the hotel bill."

"You mean she kept it all in her room?"

"She didn't want to. She wanted to hand it over to the hotel for safe-keeping, but there was never anyone at the desk when she went. She spoke to the hall porter, but he said it was nothing to do with him and wouldn't help, so she stopped trying. In any case she didn't feel that these were people she could trust.

"We didn't bring very much money. We thought we could stay in Lee's apartment, but it was too far away from the hospital and not big enough for three of us.

There's only—'' Maria checked herself and said, smiling, "But of course you already know this."

"Actually I've never been to Lee's apartment," Diana said hastily. "We'd only just met before this happened. You may find that hard to believe, but I promise you it's true."

"Oh no," Maria said wisely. "I don't find it hard to believe at all. It was the same with my Giorgio. After the very first meeting I was sure this was the man for me—of course I knew we'd fight, which we do. But I also knew I couldn't live without him." She regarded Diana with new interest. "And so it was that way with you and my brother? I shall never again believe that the English are a cold people."

"You're jumping to conclusions," Diana protested, aware than she was blushing. "It wasn't exactly like that—" She stopped, remembering the torrent of passion that had carried her away and wondering whom she was trying to fool.

Maria patted her arm. "I know. We try to tell ourselves that we're still in control, but in our hearts we know better. It's no use to fight it."

"Perhaps you'd better finish telling me about your troubles," Diana said hastily.

"Yes. We found this little hotel where we could stay. It's a horrible place but it's near the hospital. Now our money has gone, and the hotel manager practically accused us of lying. He thinks there was no money and it's a trick to get out of the bill. Mama is so upset she can't stop crying, but she doesn't want Lee to know in case he worries."

"She's right," Diana said thoughtfully. "First thing, have you reported the theft to the police?"

Maria shook her head. "I want to, but my parents are afraid. The manager says he will tell the police it's all lies, and they will be angry with us."

A little wail from inside Lee's room made them look around quickly. "That's Mama," Maria said. "She must have broken down."

They went back to find Mama sitting on the edge of the bed, sobbing in her son's arms. Lee was patting her back, and his face was full of helpless frustration. "If only I could get out of here to sort this out," he growled.

"No, no, you must stay and get well," his mother said with a little shriek. "I never meant to tell you…"

"Of course you had to tell me, Mama," he said soothingly. "And you must report this at once."

"But suppose the police believe that man's lies?" she protested. "They may put us in jail."

Lee hugged her reassuringly. "Of course they won't. Mama, I'm surprised at you. How can you think so badly of policemen when I'm one myself."

"But you're Italian," his mother wept. "It's different."

"Look, there's nothing to worry about," Diana said. "*I'm* going to sort this out."

Lee looked up at her quickly with a telling expression of passionate gratitude that went to her heart. He squeezed her hand. "If there's one person in the world I'm glad to have on my side right now, it's you," he said. "It's all right, Mama. Diana is a lawyer. She can deal with anyone."

"What's the name of the hotel?" Diana asked.

"The Sherwood," Maria told her. "It's on Penhurst Street."

"Then your nearest police station will be Penhurst Green," Lee said. "It's a pity I don't know anyone there."

"Never mind. We'll manage perfectly well without you," Diana informed him. "I'd better go and see about it now. Perhaps Maria could come with me and your parents could stay here?"

Everyone agreed to this plan, and Lee gave her hand another squeeze before she left, saying, "Promise to come back."

"Of course." She kissed him lightly, then left with Maria.

On the journey Lee's sister filled in the details. "I kept the money in a cupboard by my bed. It's all gone, even the envelope."

"Was the cupboard locked?" Diana asked.

"Yes, I made sure of that."

"Did the lock look as though it had been forced?"

"No. Whoever had done it must have had a key because it had been locked again afterward. But the manager says this proves we are lying."

"More likely it was one of the staff who stole the envelope," Diana explained. "Tell me some more about the hall porter. I don't like the sound of him."

"He's a horrible man. His name is Mr. Philips. When Mama was asking him to put our money in the safe he wanted to know how much it was, and Mama showed him everything she had in an attempt to make him realize how important it was. But he just shrugged and said there wasn't enough money to worry about."

"Did he indeed?" Diana said thoughtfully.

"He said, 'There are perfectly good cupboards in your rooms. Just use one and don't come troubling me.'"

"So it was at his suggestion that the money was put where it was? That's very important."

"But he denies it," Maria said despairingly. "He says he never talked to Mama, never saw the money, never said anything about the cupboards."

"Well, he would, wouldn't he?"

"Suddenly you sound cheerful," Maria said, mystified.

"Let's just say a thought has occurred to me. We'll go to the hotel first. What's the manager's name, by the way?"

"Mr. Beezley."

"We'll give Mr. Beezley one last chance to behave decently. If he doesn't—and I don't suppose he will—we'll go to the police ourselves."

Mr. Beezley turned out to be as down-at-heel and unprepossessing as the establishment he ran with a conspicuous lack of efficiency. There was no one on the desk when they entered. Diana had to ring the bell three times before she got an answer. She used the interval to look around the lobby and locate a fire exit, which turned out to be locked.

The manager finally arrived, belligerent and unhelpful, repeating in a yelping voice that there had been no theft and the whole thing was a trick to get out of paying the bill. He was a thoroughly unpleasant man, and Diana had no compunction about what she was about to do to him. "For the last time, will you call the police or must we do it?" she demanded.

"For the last time, you can go to the devil, all of you. And don't tell me this lot are going to call the police because they wouldn't dare. Load of thieving foreigners. Think they can come here and deceive honest people."

"All right, you've had your chance," Diana said. "Maria, I'd like to see your room."

"You won't find any evidence of theft," Beezley snapped. "Because there hasn't been one."

"I'm not looking for evidence of theft," Diana informed him coolly. "I'm looking for evidence of defective safety precautions. I'll find those sure enough."

She was on her way up the stairs before he could find an answer to this. As she had supposed, the hotel was a fire trap, with two more emergency exits blocked. "Even if you wanted to come back here I wouldn't let you," she observed as she looked around. Then, catching sight of Maria's look of surprise, she added self-consciously, "I didn't mean to sound bossy. It's just that—well, I guess it comes with being a lawyer. I get used to telling people what's best for them." She tried to sound casual. "Perhaps I do it too much."

"Don't be so serious," Maria chided her. "How can I blame you when you are so good to us?"

"Let's get on to the police," Diana said hurriedly.

They found Penhurst Green police station three streets away, and here their luck was in. While they were explaining the problem to the desk sergeant, a door into a rear room was opened. There stood a large middle-aged man who looked like a haystack. He called to the sergeant, "It's about time you—*well*, if it isn't Miss Waldman!"

"Detective Inspector Lorrimer!" she exclaimed. "Of course, we encountered each other over that bullion fraud."

"Yes, you made mincemeat of a perfectly good prosecution case," he grumbled without rancor, shaking her hand.

"If it had been perfectly good, I couldn't have made mincemeat of it," she said, smiling.

"Well, I bear no grudge. It taught me to be more careful about details. Come inside and tell me what brings you to this part of the world."

They followed him into an interview room where he ordered tea and Diana told the story. "I'm pretty certain that porter is the thief," she said, "in fact, I wouldn't mind betting he's done it before."

"Well, it's easy enough to check if he's on file," Lorrimer said. He called someone on the internal phone and five minutes later a young constable appeared carrying several large volumes, which he set on the table before Maria. They contained hundreds of pictures of men who roughly corresponded to her description of the porter. "See if you can spot him in the beauty parade," Lorrimer told her.

After ten minutes of flicking over pages Maria said, "That's him."

"'Tufty' Ardrick," Lorrimer said.

"In the hotel he's known as Mr. Philips," Maria said, "but it's the same man."

"He's crossed my path before," Lorrimer recalled. "He's a petty thief, gets employed at hotels where they can't afford to be careful about the staff and supplements his pay with various petty dishonesties. He's done quite a bit of time in short sentences. Did you let on that you suspected him, Miss Waldman?"

"Of course not," she said indignantly. "I'm not that naive."

"No, I should have guessed. Right then, he's probably still there, thinking he's got away with it. Give me five minutes to get the search warrant, then we'll be on our way."

"While you're doing that I'd like to make a quick phone call."

"Be my guest."

They met outside five minutes later and returned to the hotel. The first thing that met their eyes was Mr. Philips on the desk. He was a short, scrawny individual with a bullying face that set into apprehensive lines as soon as he saw them. "Afternoon Tufty," the inspector said with dreadful geniality. "Been up to your old tricks again?"

"I don't care what lies she's been telling you," Tufty squealed. "You can't pin this one on me."

"Well, why don't we have a look through your room?" Lorrimer suggested.

"You can't do that without a search warrant. Bet you ain't got one."

Lorrimer seemed to regard the unpleasant little man more in sorrow than in anger. "Tufty, you underestimate me."

Beezley appeared, adding his fourpenceworth of bluster, but the sight of Lorrimer's official badge reduced him to stammers. A search of Tufty's room revealed the missing money, still in the brown envelope in which Maria had stored it. Lorrimer briskly arrested the culprit, handcuffed him, and led him downstairs to the lobby.

Maria was almost tearful with relief. "When will I get the money back?" she asked Lorrimer.

"Not for a while I'm afraid," he said. "It's evidence."

"But how shall we pay our bill?"

"I doubt if Mr. Beezley will have the nerve to charge you when it was his own negligence that brought this about," Diana hinted.

Beezley flung her a malevolent look, as he pointed to a notice over the desk. "'This hotel takes no responsibility for customer's possessions unless they are placed in the hotel safe,'" he quoted.

"But the hotel staff refused to put it in the safe," Diana reminded him.

"Prove it," he snapped.

She sighed. "I see how it is. The two of you are in it together. You were going to share the loot afterward."

"Do you think so?" Lorrimer said, sounding interested.

"I'm sure of it."

"Now look," Beezley said hastily, "I don't want any trouble. I'm willing—purely as a gesture of goodwill—to write off the bill. It's without prejudice—meaning I admit nothing."

"My client accepts your generous offer," Diana informed him witheringly. "Also without prejudice—meaning I still think you're as guilty as hell."

"What was that about your 'client'?" he demanded.

"Didn't I tell you I was a lawyer? Never mind. You've found out now, haven't you?"

"You shouldn't have taken her on, old son," Lorrimer advised the wretched Beezley. "She had me once for breakfast. You wouldn't even make a satisfying mouthful."

"A highly distasteful one," Diana confirmed. "Maria, please go and do your packing while I wait here. Mr. Beezley is going to give me a receipt for your bill."

Recognizing the voice of authority Maria hurried away to comply. Lorrimer looked worried. "I need to

know where the family will be staying,'' he said.
''They're witnesses.''

''Don't worry, they'll be staying with me,'' Diana
told him.

After Lorrimer returned to the station with his
prisoner, Diana helped Maria pile her family's lug-
gage into her car. As she was starting the engine another car drew up quickly outside the hotel, two men
got out and hurried in. Diana waited a moment before pulling away from the curb, but not before she
had the satisfaction of hearing Beezley's bellow of
dismay and outrage as he discovered his visitors'
identities. She drove on with a quiet smile on her face.
Maria noticed it but said nothing.

On arrival at the police station Maria's first action
was to ask for a phone to let her parents know that all
was well again. Diana moved away to give her some
privacy. After a few minutes Maria came to find her.
''Mama says we must go back quickly so that she can
tell you herself how grateful she is.''

''We'll return as soon as you've given your statement to the inspector,'' Diana said as they rejoined
Lorrimer.

Maria told her story again while a constable took it
down and when he'd read it back to her, she agreed
that it was accurate and signed it. ''I'd like you to
bring your parents in tomorrow morning for their
statements,'' he said to Maria.

''Is that necessary?'' Maria asked anxiously. ''It will
worry them so dreadfully. Won't my statement do?''

''I'm afraid not,'' Lorrimer said kindly. ''I need
statements from everyone involved.''

''Would it help if I came too?'' Diana said.

"Oh yes," Maria said eagerly. "Mama thinks you're a kind of magician already. She'll feel safe with you."

"Can you put it off for a day, Inspector?" Diana suggested. "I'm in court tomorrow."

"No problem," he said easily.

As they were driving back to the hospital Maria said, "Diana, who were those two men who came to the hotel as we were leaving?"

"They were the people I sent for when I made that phone call," Diana said.

"But who were they? And why did Mr. Beezley yell?"

"They were marshalls from the fire department with power to close that death trap down if necessary. And that's why he yelled."

Maria gave a rich crow of laughter. "I see that my brother was right about you."

"Why, what did he say?

"Not yet. I'll tell you one day."

"Tell me now."

"No." Maria chuckled again and nodded, "But he was right."

Six

As they drove up outside the hospital Diana said, "I took the liberty of telling the inspector that you and your parents would be staying with me for a while."

"That's very kind of you, but won't we crowd your house out?"

"Not a chance. It's much too big for me."

They hurried to Lee's room. Mama and Papa looked up eagerly as they went in, and Mama immediately went to Diana and threw her arms about her. "Maria has told us that you work miracles," she said.

"Not miracles," Diana disclaimed hastily. "Just a matter of going to the local police. Luckily they had the thief on file and the rest was easy."

"Mama, you and Papa must go to the station to make statements," Maria said. "But don't worry because Diana will go with you. She even made the police wait a day so that she could be there."

"I didn't *make* them do it," Diana said, alarmed by her elevation to the status of heroine. "Inspector Lorrimer was a very friendly man who was happy to agree. Lee will tell you that the police are always willing to be helpful over things like that. Aren't they, Lee?" she added urgently.

He was looking at her strangely. "It's true," he confirmed, adding in a lower voice to Diana, "but I can't help feeling that you would have *made* them if it had been necessary." He drew her near. "Thank you," he said softly. "You don't know what it means to me to see my mother happy again."

"I'm going to take them back home with me," she whispered. "It's quite close for visiting, and they won't have any more trouble."

Lee looked startled. "Home? You mean to Wendle House?"

"Yes, of course. They haven't got any money because the police are holding theirs for evidence, and they need somewhere to stay, preferably near here. You've seen how enormous my place is. Why do you look like that? I thought you'd be pleased."

"I am—that is I'm grateful for all you're going—" Lee stopped, disturbed by an uneasy sensation that he couldn't explain. He only knew that he was reluctant to see his whole family become chicks under Diana's wing. And that was shocking when she was being so marvelous.

I'm an ungrateful lout, he castigated himself mentally. *But I just wish this hadn't happened.*

"Of course I'm pleased, darling," he told her firmly. "I'm delighted. My only problem is that I'm going to sink so deeply in your debt that I'll vanish altogether."

"But I don't see it as a debt," she said, puzzled. She wondered why he couldn't understand that what she did for him was a pleasure, that she felt close to him. Surely he felt the same? He'd spent the week babbling about her in his unconsciousness. That must prove something. But a little chill of dismay had taken hold of her heart.

Maria was explaining the new arrangement to her parents. Mama was joyful but not, apparently, much surprised. She seemed to consider Diana already one of the family. "We will be no trouble," she promised. "We will look after the house and the cooking."

"Well, you can fight that out with Vita," Diana said, smiling.

"Vita?" Mama beamed with comprehension. "She is your aunt perhaps, or your cousin, who keeps your house while you are away being a lawyer?"

"Well, she does look after me, but we're not related. She's just a friend. So is Martin who runs the garden."

"Your family don't do these things?" Mama queried, puzzled.

"I have no family," Diana said.

Mama responded sympathetically by crushing her in another bear hug and said, "You have a family now." Then she began to chivvy the other two toward the door, announcing portentously, "It is time for us to go to the canteen."

Maria and her father exchanged knowing grins and dutifully followed her out of the room without a word, leaving Lee and Diana feeling self-conscious. "My mother means to be the soul of tact," he said with a smile. He drew her close. "What can I say to you? They would have been lost without you."

"Don't say anything. Kiss me," she pleaded.

When they could speak again he said slightly breathlessly, "I wish I could be a fly on the wall when my mother descends on Vita."

"Yes, I know what you mean." She smiled. "It'll be lovely having them."

"Beware. You may end up with three more permanently in the house. Then I shall have to move in, too."

"It's a big house," she said invitingly. It was partly a joke, but the thought of Lee always around the place had its own charm. But he didn't take her up on the remark, choosing instead to let the moment pass.

That evening she drove the family to Wendle House, having first called Vita and Martin to prepare them. She'd had a few qualms about how everyone would get on together, and considered asking Vita to modify some of her more lurid reminiscences out of consideration for Mama's respectable ears. Deciding against it still made her feel as though she was on hot coals.

From the moment they arrived it was plain that Vita was on her best behavior. She'd toned down her appearance, assuming a more reserved mien of admirable gravity as she showed the arrivals to their rooms, which bore fresh spring flowers that looked bright and welcoming. The only awkwardness was caused by Fang who'd slipped into Mama and Papa's bedroom and sprawled out in lordly fashion on one of the twin beds. Vita's instructions to him to make himself scarce fell on deaf ears, and only a command from Diana produced any result.

"I apologize for the contretemps," Vita asserted with a formality that told Diana she was watching every word. For a startled moment she wondered if her

old friend had picked up her worries telepathically.
She couldn't know of Martin's instruction to Vita to
"do yourself up a bit. This is important to Di," or
Vita's lofty rejoinder, "You don't have to tell me it's
important that *his* parents are coming to stay. How
about you bringing in a bit less of the garden on your
boots for a change?"

When Diana went in later to make sure they were all
right, she found Maria helping them with their un-
packing. The chest of drawers was adorned by a pho-
tograph of a boy and girl in their teens, both bearing
a striking resemblance to Lee. Mama explained that
these were Antonia and Carlo.

"You must miss them a lot," Diana said, smiling.

"They are staying with my brother's family," Mama
said. "They're in good hands but—yes, we miss
them."

"I expect you'd like to telephone to tell them you've
moved."

To her surprise the old people looked embarrassed,
and Mama cast an unhappy glance at Maria, who
seemed to be the family spokesperson. "A call like
that is expensive," Maria said, "and now we have no
money—"

"Give me the number and I'll get it for you," Diana
said firmly.

A few minutes later the call was made and Mama
was chattering eagerly to Antonia. When she'd hung
up she enfolded Diana in a massive embrace, which
she followed by erupting into the kitchen, demanding
to be given some work to do.

Over supper the atmosphere relaxed. Mama and
Vita recognized in each other kindred spirits in the
kitchen, and by the time they'd swapped a couple of

recipes over a bottle of wine Mama had relaxed enough to hear Vita's jail stories in a sympathetic spirit. Papa and Martin found a common bond in football. Clive tried to flirt with Maria, but she snubbed him firmly, pretending to talk to Diana whom she plainly regarded as a potential sister.

"I hope we won't trouble you long," she said.

"It's no trouble. I love having you," Diana told her truthfully.

"You have saved us in so many ways. Now that Lee is out of danger I should go home to my husband. Before this I had to stay for Mama and Papa. They too should be returning to Antonia and Carlo. Now I think they'll go with easier minds because we leave Lee in your hands." Her face brightened, "Now I will tell you what he said about you."

"Yes, what was it?" Diana asked eagerly.

"He said you were a slayer of dragons. The more dragons you found to slay the better you were pleased. And I can see it's true, because you like to look after people." She embraced Diana impulsively. "I'm going to like having you as a sister."

"Well I—I don't know," Diana said, embarrassed.

Maria laughed at her discomfiture. "But *I* do."

As she was going to bed that night Diana stopped on the landing and listened to the house humming about her. She could hear Mama and Papa coming upstairs, talking in low voices, and Maria and Vita chatting in Maria's room. The house seemed warmer and more full of light than she ever remembered it being, and some of that warmth and light had become part of her. This pleasant human buzz was what Lee had always had, shielding him from the loneliness of the world, and just by coming into her life he'd brought some of its rich glow with him.

She remembered how large and cold the house had seemed in her own childhood. The stairs had seemed to stretch up a great distance into the darkness. Actually they'd merely stretched up to the neat corner room that had become hers.

At fourteen she'd persuaded her grandfather to let her change rooms, saying she needed more space. But her real reason had been her dislike to the corner room and its memories. Even now it sometimes seemed as if only a fine line separated her from the anguished child of those days.

Impulsively she went along the corridor to her old room. It was the first time she'd been there in years. It looked dreary, the bed had been stripped, the walls looked naked as there were no pictures or decorations, but even when it had been full of her possessions it had left a bleak impression in her memory. A heaviness fell on her heart as she stood in the doorway fighting the impulse to run away. She walked over to the window and looked out. It was as she recalled. There was a strong drainpipe leading down to where the roof jutted out to touch the branches of a tree. It was an easy descent, as the ten-year-old Diana had discovered long ago on the night she'd run away from this house.

No one ever knew she'd gone. A few hours later she'd returned the way she'd come, slipping quietly into bed and lying as still and cold as a stone, hating the world for the betrayal she had suffered but refusing to let her grief spill over into tears. Since then she had hardly ever cried.

Somewhere behind her she heard a scream of laughter from Lee's mother. She left, shutting the door on her painful musings, then rushed to his parents' room where Fang was once more ensconced on one of the beds, resisting the combined efforts of Papa, Maria and Clive to remove him. "Off," she commanded, and he vanished.

Mama told the story of their arrival to find him in possession, with cries and gesticulations, and in the general laughter Diana discovered that the little corner room had faded again, until she could almost believe it had all been a bad dream.

She didn't see Lee until the evening of next day. The family greeted her as an old friend as soon as she arrived, but then Mama announced, with her usual heavy-handed tact, that the family was departing for the canteen. As soon as the door had closed Lee and Diana rocked with laughter. "My poor Papa," Lee choked. "He hates the canteen coffee and he's practically got it running out of his ears."

"I love your parents," Diana said warmly. "Vita told me this morning that she found their twin beds pushed together. They apologized for disturbing her arrangements, but said they couldn't sleep if they were apart."

"Of course. It's the Italian way. We don't believe in your cold, English sleeping arrangements. Married people belong together."

"How are you feeling now?"

"Much better."

"Good, then I have a bone to pick with you." Lee set his face in lines of mock horror. "How dare you set Clive on to be my watchdog."

Lee grimaced. "What on earth possessed him to tell you about that?"

"He didn't have a lot of choice after he stopped Gavin's left hook."

She described how Clive had followed her and suffered for it, and Lee grinned. "I'll have to make it up to him. Come on, I didn't do anything so terrible."

"You told him I was bossy. That's terrible."

"I didn't *precisely* say you were bossy," he hedged. "If you were to examine every word I uttered with care, considering all the implications and taking into account every possible shade of meaning—well anyway, you are bossy. Now stop arguing and kiss me."

When visiting time was over the family returned to bid him good-night. A nurse came in during the farewells, wearing a look of disapproval. "You shouldn't really have this number of people here, Inspector," she said. "It isn't good for you."

"We're just leaving," Diana said hastily.

"Good," the nurse announced glacially, and retired.

Lee ground his teeth in frustration. "I can't wait to get out of this place."

Diana nodded sympathetically. "Yes, if you're a bossy person used to giving orders it's hard to get used to taking them."

He glared at her. "They're planning to send me to some damned convalescent home for a month," he growled.

"Well, that needn't be so bad," Diana said.

"You don't know the one they have in mind. It's part nursing home, part old people's home. I'll have to spend my time 'relaxing' in a bath chair on the terrace, playing Scrabble with retired colonels. I'll go crazy.''

"Then don't go," Diana said.

"That's easy to say, but they won't let me out of here until I can be sure of constant proper attention."

"And they're right," Mama declared. "You don't go back to work before you're ready. The people at the nursing home will make you behave yourself."

"I'm not ten years old, Mama," Lee declared wrathfully.

"No, you just act it."

"Actually there's no need for you to play Scrabble with retired colonels," Diana said suddenly. "I know where you can get constant attention without going to a nursing home."

"Where? Where?" Lee said at once.

"But you don't have to ask. You gave me the idea yourself. Come to Wendle House."

"Oh no. Di, that's out of the question. I've taken enough from you."

"But it's the ideal solution. Vita will love mother henning you."

"That Vita is a good woman," Mama declared.

"She's a splendid woman," Lee conceded, "but I don't want to be mother henned by her or anyone."

"You have to be looked after by someone," Diana pointed out. "It's either Vita and me or the nursing home."

Lee groaned. Part of him was unwilling to continue letting Diana see him looking helpless, but part of him was thinking what it would be like to be with her day after day.

It was Mama who made the decision for him. "If we know you are well looked after, we can return to our other children," she said. "I should be with Antonia. She has started going out with an unsuitable boy."

"At her age?" Lee demanded, scandalized.

Maria chuckled with malicious enjoyment. "When you were her age you'd already—"

"Yes, never mind that," Lee interrupted hastily. "Mama, of course you must go back to the children."

"So it's all settled," Mama announced. She gave Diana a smacking kiss. "If you are going to look after my Lee, I must tell you everything he likes and the things that put him in a bad mood, that you will need to know—"

"She won't need to know that at all," Lee growled. "My mood is always perfect."

"Ha! Listen to him. On the day of your wedding I will weep, not with joy but with surprise that you found a nice woman to put up with you."

Then, having embarrassed everyone about equally, Mama beamed around and said, "Now, shall we go home?"

Diana's next duty, and her most difficult one, was to explain to Hugh that she wouldn't be going to Lake Como. She met him in a bar one evening, hoping to let him down as lightly as she could, but she balked at giving him the real reason because the magic that was growing between herself and Lee was too precious to be touched by words. "I don't think it would be fair to do anything that might give Leila false hopes," she said gently.

"Is that your way of telling me that you won't marry me?" Hugh asked.

"I suppose it is. Hugh, dear, it really wouldn't have worked. If it had been right for us to marry, I wouldn't have needed to take this long making up my mind. I dallied too long with the idea because you're so terribly suitable." Her wry smile made a mockery of herself.

"I thought you cared for me, Diana," he said gruffly, not looking at her.

"I do, but not like that. I thought the way I felt might be enough, but it isn't. I should have known better."

"It seems that I'm the person who didn't know you," he said stiffly. "You've always been so sane and sensible. Now you're telling me that you've fallen in love with someone who *isn't* suitable."

"I didn't say that at all," she protested in dismay.

"Give me credit for a little perception, my dear. When a woman starts saying that once she thought a certain kind of love was enough and now she knows it isn't, it means she's fallen in love." Diana was silent, unable to answer, and Hugh persisted, "He isn't suitable, is he?"

"I don't know what he is, really," she said softly, "except that—" She returned to reality to discover that her hand was pressed revealingly over her heart, a self-conscious gesture that Hugh could not ignore.

"I see what it is," he said. "It's not unknown for terribly sensible women to suddenly throw their hats over the windmill. You've become infatuated with one of your refuge tramps, haven't you."

To her own annoyance Diana couldn't repress a gasp at how close he'd come to the truth. She was glad the dim light hid her burning cheeks.

"Well, have your little fling my dear," Hugh said. "I can be patient."

"You mean you'd take me back after my *little fling*?" she asked curiously.

"You said yourself that we're *suitable* together. At one time you'd have been the first to say that's what really matters in marriage."

"Would I? Yes, I suppose I would have."

"When you've got it out of your system, I'll be waiting."

"Don't wait, Hugh," she said, rising to leave. "I won't be coming back."

As she had anticipated, Vita was delighted at the prospect of having Lee to stay. She listened solemnly to the multitude of instructions Mama gave her and promised to be a second mother to him. The Fortuno family returned to Italy with light hearts, waved off at the airport by Diana.

Summer had come and the courts had broken up for the recess. Her time was her own, to spend as much of it with Lee as she liked. She drove home from the airport in a state of light-headed happiness such as she'd known few times in her life. She began counting off the occasions: passing her exams with honors, being called to the bar, winning her first case.

Each time her grandfather had taken her to dinner, sometimes introducing her to his colleagues with barely restrained pride. He'd praised her in his solemn way, and she'd felt an immense satisfaction at having measured up to his high standards. Now she discovered that that satisfaction palled to insignificance next to the joyous glow that possessed her at the thought of being with Lee.

A bedroom had been made up for him on the ground floor, with French windows leading out onto the big garden. An ambulance brought him to Wendle House two days later. He walked in determinedly on his own feet, but the effort took its toll and when Vita insisted that he rest he didn't argue.

Over the next few days he gained strength and was often to be found in the kitchen, peeling potatoes for Vita, or teaching her Italian recipes. But he tired quickly, usually agreeing to spend the afternoon lounging on the shaded garden seat.

He rapidly became an object of interest to the three children next door. Their own garden was a lot smaller, and they liked nothing better than to slip through the fence to have more space for their games. Diana would have turned a blind eye, but Martin grew wrathful if he saw them and moaned so bitterly about the hazards to his flowers and vegetables that she gave in for the sake of a quiet life.

But Lee proved an attraction that even fear of Martin couldn't overcome. Through the mysterious operations of the grapevine, the children soon learned that he was a police officer wounded by criminals. When he appeared in the garden they would hurry over to demand stories of gangland villainy, the more lurid the better. To Diana's amusement Lee seemed to enjoy entertaining them, and his tales were as color-ful as the most bloodthirsty child could hope for.

"I'm sure it's not good for them to have you pander to their fantasies like that," Diana chuckled one evening as she was lazing on the seat, happily ensconced in the circle of his arms, while they swung gently back and forth.

"Nonsense," he said cheerfully. "Children are natural ghouls. Besides, none of it's real to them. I edit out the disturbing bits and just pile on lots of dead bodies."

"Aren't dead bodies disturbing?"

"Not like cruelty and meanness," he said thoughtfully. "When you see old ladies beaten up for a couple of pounds, or just for the pleasure of it—*that's* disturbing. You see their faces covered in ugly bruises, and their eyes full of bewilderment because they don't understand how the world can do such a thing to them—then you get the suspect in and you have to treat him with kid gloves—" He broke off with a little shudder.

"Then what?" Diana asked, frowning.

"Then I sometimes wish I could take the gloves off and show them what it feels like," Lee finished. "Those are the cases I'd never tell children about. But on a 'bang-you're-dead' level, it's just a harmless game."

"Have you ever taken the kid gloves off?" Diana asked after a brief hesitation.

Lee shrugged. "I lost my temper once with a lout who'd kicked an old man's head in. He knew he was pretty safe. The only witness was the victim's wife, who was too upset to identify him properly. He sat there in the police station laughing at me. I saw red and pitched into him. He was basically a coward, and it was enough to scare him. He admitted everything, but then he hired a lawyer who specialized in cases of police brutality. The charge was thrown out, I was officially reprimanded, and he, on the other hand, ended up back on the streets, free to kick more heads in." He saw her troubled frown and said firmly, "The only thing I'm ashamed of is that he went free. Let's not pursue it. We're never going to see eye-to-eye on this subject.''

''Because I'm the kind of lawyer you hate?'' she queried. ''The kind who thinks 'all coppers are pigs and all villains are saints'?''

''I wouldn't put it quite like that,'' he began.

''But you did put it like that when we first met,'' she reminded him. ''You accused me of taking you up because you had some bruises and I could use you for a bit of police brutality. 'Cannon fodder' was your exact expression.''

''Well,'' he said uneasily, ''there are one or two lawyers who fit that description. I've learned since that you're a lot more complicated. Besides, I was trying to get rid of you. I knew you spelled trouble.'' He tightened his arm, drawing her close. Diana kissed him gently, then more urgently as she felt the leap of his desire. Her own surged to meet it, but she reluctantly disengaged herself. ''What's the matter?'' he asked with a touch of mischief. ''Afraid I'll have a collapse?''

''Something like that,'' she said in an unsteady voice.

He sighed. ''I can see my convalescence is going to be a great trial to both of us. You're not sorry you brought me here, are you?''

''Yes and no,'' she replied thoughtfully. ''I think it's time we went in for supper.''

''I don't think Martin's speaking to me. One of the kids lost his ball in the middle of a row of lettuces this afternoon. I offered to pay for any damage, but I don't think I placated him.''

"I should think not. Those lettuces are the pride of his life. Vita always offers to let you have supper in bed. Why not take it that way tonight?"

"Stop protecting me. I'll brave Martin's wrath."

Vita had made a splendid salad, dressed up with some Italian tips from Lee. Everyone enjoyed it, but Martin couldn't resist observing gloomily that it would have been improved with a bit more lettuce. "But I'm afraid we're going to be short of lettuces this year," he added with a dark glance at the culprit.

"Would you like me to commit suicide now or will later do?" Lee asked innocently.

"You hush up," Vita commented, "and I mean both of you."

"I'm beginning to see why you got on so well with my mother," he said. "You're just like her."

"Treat me with some respect then," Vita suggested.

But Lee's face was suddenly gray, and all the willpower in the world couldn't stop him closing his eyes as weariness swept over him in a wave. "I think I'll go to bed after all," he said.

Diana rose quickly to help him, but Clive offered his arm at the same time and it was to Clive that he turned. "Thank you anyway, darling," he said to soften the rejection.

"I don't mean half the things I say," Martin declared suddenly.

"Sure you don't," Lee told him, resting a hand briefly on Martin's shoulder before Clive led him out.

When Diana looked in on Lee half an hour later he was sleeping soundly. He still looked exhausted, and she made a private resolve not to let him overtax his strength in future.

Seven

Over the next few weeks Diana's determination to guard Lee often clashed with his determination not to be "mollycoddled." There were frequent squabbles because they were both strong-willed, but they always ended up in each other's arms.

Diana became aware that Lee really was improving fast by the increasing strength of his embrace and the ardor of his kisses. He would kiss her mischievously, murmuring, "Does that feel like an invalid?" and the dizzying desire would riot in her, making it harder and harder for her to draw back. But she always did, fearful of the damage it might do him if they yielded to their passion.

One day she went to his home to collect his mail. She had volunteered for the job because she was eager to see where he lived. He was housed on the fifth floor in a small, neat apartment that was austerely furnished. The surroundings would have been bleak except for the photographs of his family that were in profusion. His bedroom was small and contained a narrow bed, a wardrobe, some books and family portraits. Studying them, Diana saw a crowd of faces that must be brothers, sisters, parents, grandparents and grandchildren. Maria was there with her husband Giorgio, and another sea of faces that was presumably Giorgio's family.

On Lee's bedside table Diana discovered a book labeled Birthdays. Opening it she found it was a diary containing the birth dates of everyone in the extended family, plus a note to say how old each would be this year. Fascinated, she counted them and found 150. She sat on the bed, awed by such family solidarity, but warmed by it too.

She drove home, longing to talk to Lee, but as she turned into her drive she groaned, pulled up short by the sight of Hugh's car. She hurried in but Clive intercepted her in the hall, his finger to his lips. "This way," he whispered, "and don't make a sound."

He led her to Lee's room, where the French windows stood open. Martin and Vita were standing there looking like gleeful children, and they beckoned her forward with further injunctions to silence. "Out there," Vita whispered, pointing to where Diana could just make out the swinging seat. Lee was sitting on it listening to Hugh, who was standing over him in a hectoring manner.

"I hope you appreciate how lucky you've been, young man," Hugh was saying.

And to Diana's astonishment Lee replied in a humble voice, "Miss Waldman has been very good to me, sir."

"Miss Waldman is very good to a lot of people, and she should know better. She picks up the riffraff of society at that place, then she fills her home with them, giving you all the perfect opportunity to take advantage of her."

"Who does he think he's talking about?" Martin snapped. "If I was twenty years younger, I'd give him riffraff!"

"I don't think I was taking advantage of her, sir," Lee replied in the same humble tone.

"You forget that I happen to know you're a petty crook. I first saw you in the dock, which is where your kind belongs. But I suppose Miss Waldman got you off. She specializes in hopeless cases."

"No, sir, I wouldn't let her help me, not wanting to impose on her goodness."

Diana's lips twitched at Lee's wicked joke. "But even Hugh won't fall for that line," she said quietly.

"Wanna bet?" Vita murmured.

It seemed she was right. Hugh declared loftily, "I'm glad you have that much sense of decency. You didn't cut a very prepossessing figure that day, I can tell you."

"No, sir, the judge thought the same. He sent me down for three months, but I got time off for good behavior," Lee added quickly, as though trying to placate his accuser. "I learned my lesson, you see."

"If you ask me, the only lesson you learned is how to sponge off gullible women."

"Damned cheek!" Diana exclaimed. Beside her, Vita, Martin, and Clive were doubled up in silent laughter.

"Miss Waldman rescued me," Lee explained. "She thought I had possibilities."

"And you reward her faith in you by loafing around in her garden as though you had nothing to do but be waited on," Hugh growled. "Look at you, lounging there when I'm talking to you. Get up, man!"

Before any of the spectators realized what he was going to do, he reached forward and grabbed Lee, yanking him firmly to his feet. Horrified, Diana sprinted across the lawn. "Stop it, Hugh," she said frantically. "He's wounded."

But there was no need to say it. The movement had dragged Lee's shirt open, revealing an ugly red line across his chest where the bandages had recently been removed.

"For pity's sake, Diana," Lee said, exasperated, "Will you stop acting like my mother? I'm strong enough to hang this idiot up on the nearest tree by his belt, and I'm very tempted to do it."

"Hugh," she said, seeing that he was about to explode, "I don't know what Lee's told you but—"

"I didn't tell him anything," Lee said. "He just walked in here, assuming the worst."

"Well, you had no right to," Diana informed Hugh.

"You forget, my dear, that when I first encountered this person he was in the dock."

"So was your brother," she reminded him crisply, "so let's hear no more about that."

Hugh glared but refused to be distracted. "Naturally I'm sorry if I have aggravated his injury—"

"You haven't," Lee said hastily. "Don't put that idea into her head, for heaven's sake!"

"—an injury that was gained, I've no doubt, in dubious circumstances."

"When a man gets shot in the chest the circumstances are usually dubious," Lee observed mildly.

"Exactly my point."

"I was shot by a drug peddler, actually."

"There! You see!" Hugh exploded to Diana. "He admits it! What more do you need to open your eyes?"

"Hugh, please go away and stop talking nonsense. Lee is a policeman. He should have told you that."

"Why should I?" Lee demanded. "If he wants to make a clown of himself, it's not my job to stop him."

"Darling, please look after yourself properly," she begged. "I think I'd better call the doctor."

"If you do, I walk out of here and never come back," he declared wrathfully.

Hugh's eyes had narrowed. "'Darling,'" he echoed. "Do you mean to tell me—is this—?"

"Yes, Hugh, this is my windmill."

Hugh breathed hard. "I came here because I was concerned for you. It seems I was right. I wouldn't have believed it possible that you could so lose your senses."

"Neither would I," she admitted. "But I'm afraid I have."

Hugh turned his glare on Lee, but Lee was looking at Diana. "I'll go for a moment," he said. "But I'm not leaving it there. I'll be back."

"It's no use, Hugh," Diana said. "Don't try to save me. There's no hope for me at all, I'm afraid."

"I'm sure you know your way out," Lee told him pleasantly. "Don't risk staying for supper. I wouldn't answer for what Vita might put in your soup."

Hugh turned and walked off. Neither of them saw him go. "It was disgraceful of you to make fun of him," Diana said severely.

"I couldn't resist it. And I'm glad of it now. I learned some things I might not have learned otherwise."

"Such as what?" she asked, meeting his eyes.

"Such as windmill—as in Don Quixote?"

"No, windmill as in 'throw your cap over,'" she told him.

He took her face gently between his hands. "Is there really no hope for you?"

"No hope at all," she said, her heart hammering.

"Nor for me," he said, lowering his head.

Vita, on her way out to tell them supper was ready, turned smartly on her heel and returned to the kitchen.

That night Diana lay awake into the small hours, brooding on her love. She was about to drift off into sleep when a sound, somewhere in the house, made her start. She sat in the darkness, ears strained, and at last she heard it again, a moan of pain coming from the hall below. She was out of the bed in a second, flying across the room to open the door without even bothering to put on her dressing gown. She flew down the stairs, and in the darkness she could just make out a sight that almost caused her heart to stop. Lee was on the floor, groaning. "Darling," she said frantically and ran to him, dropping to her knees. "Stay there—don't move—"

He grabbed her wrist quickly. "Don't even think of calling a doctor. I don't want to have to explain to him that he was called out in the early morning hours because I stubbed my toe."

"You *what?*"

"I went to the bathroom. I didn't put the hall light on in case it awoke you. On the way back I barged into this monstrosity." He indicated a carved oak dresser. "It sent me flying."

"A stubbed toe," she echoed incredulously. "You mean that's all you—? You sound in agony."

"I *am* in agony," he said, exasperated. "It's probably crippled me for life. There ought to be a law against putting things like this in dark corners where they can attack honest citizens. If I knew a good lawyer I'd sue you."

"I'll introduce you to one tomorrow. Do you need any help back to bed?"

"I think I do. After all, it's the least you owe me after what you've done."

"Nice," she said indignantly.

He got gingerly to his feet and slipped an arm around Diana's neck. Holding on to her, he hopped back to his room and made it to the bed. When he'd swung his legs up she put the light on to examine the injured digit. "It looks all right to me," she said.

"It's being very brave," he assured her. "I think you should give it a good massage."

She sat down and took his foot onto her lap, soothing it between her hands. "And you're the man who doesn't like being mollycoddled," she scoffed.

"Like all women you fail to understand the principle," he explained patiently. "I didn't want to be mollycoddled when I'd merely been shot, but a man who's just rammed his big toe against a ten-ton oak dresser needs sympathy."

"I could call Vita," she teased.

"Thanks, but I prefer you. Ah, that's lovely. I think I'll forgive you after all."

As the first euphoria of relief died away, she found something else to worry about. Abandoning Lee's foot, she moved up the bed to sit where she could look at him more closely. "It can't have done you any good, being shaken up like that," she said, frowning.

"Stop fretting. I've healed perfectly. Look." He pulled open his pajama jacket to show her the mark that grew better every day. But her worried eyes didn't see the improvement, just the ugly red line that reminded her how close he'd come to death. The sight drove everything else out of her head. She leaned down to touch it gently with her lips, then she laid her cheek against it and rested there, hearing the soft thunder of his heart beneath.

Lee put his arms around her. "It's all right," he said. "It's over now."

"Not for me. Not ever."

She forced herself to rise and move away from him. The feel of his bare chest and the knowledge that they both were in just their night clothes was too dangerously sweet. Her own nightgown was flimsy and plunged so far in front that she felt naked.

"Come back," Lee commanded from the bed.

She shook her head. "No, I'd better not."

"Darling, sooner or later you are going to have to admit that I'm well again."

"That's not what you said a moment ago."

"I was joking, and you know it. I'm as strong as I ever was. Come here and let me show you."

When she didn't respond, he rose from the bed and came to stand behind her, letting his hands rest on her shoulders. She could feel his warm breath on the back of her neck.

"Lee no—please—" Diana tried to get free of him, but he quickly turned her to face him, overcoming her resistance until he had her firmly locked within the circle of his arms.

"Do you still think I'm a weakling?" he demanded, his eyes glinting with mischief.

"Your muscles seem in good working order," she conceded, trying not to sound breathless. "Now will you let me go?"

"What's the matter? Have I suddenly grown two heads? Or is there something my best friend hasn't told me?"

"Of course not."

"Then why this urgent need to get away from me? Don't my kisses please you anymore?" Without waiting for her to answer he dropped his head, coaxing her to respond. He began to trace the outline of her lips with the tip of his tongue. "Is *that* what you don't like?" he murmured.

"Oh yes," she gasped through the tremors that racked her. "I simply hate that. You know I do."

"Mm. I thought so. And you're not too keen on this either, are you?" He began inflicting sweet torture on the place just below her ear, caressing her with the skill born of much practice.

"That's right," Diana gasped, trying not to abandon all self-restraint. "I strongly disapprove of that, so why don't you stop doing it?"

He chuckled against her skin. "I guess I just enjoy your funny way of showing disapproval. You could always try pushing me away."

"I don't think that would work," she said anxiously, clinging to him.

"Mm, you're dead right. Suppose I just keep on kissing you until I find out where I'm going wrong?

Perhaps it's this?'' He made a trail of small kisses along her jawline, then farther down her neck.

Diana yielded helplessly to the sweet sensation, twining her fingers in his hair, moaning softly with pleasure. ''You're a devil,'' she told him.

''Then why are you smiling?''

''I'm just being nice about it,'' she murmured.

Lee tightened his arms around her as he fastened his mouth hard on hers. Diana knew she should think of his health, but the marvelous feel of his lips drove everything else from her mind. All she wanted was to surrender to the passion that flowed between them like an electric current. She would allow herself just one kiss and be strong afterward.

She wasn't sure whether she'd decided to part her lips or whether he'd insisted. They were so completely in harmony that the thought of one was the action of the other. But, however it happened, his tongue was suddenly in her mouth, conjuring up memories of past delight and torturing her with allurements that she must resist.

He drew the tip across the silky inner surface, sending sweet messages along nerves already stretched taut with longing. Her whole body throbbed with response. She knew she was playing a dangerous game, testing her own control to the limit. But she loved him so overwhelmingly that in the end she would find the strength to deny herself the fulfillment she craved.

But she'd been right when she said Lee was a devil. It was as though he'd divined her intentions and was set on making things as difficult as possible. He kissed her in the way she loved, slowly and with infinite gentleness, keeping a delicate balance between teasing and reassuring, until her good intentions began to slip away. There was wicked subtlety in his lips as they caressed hers. "I'm glad to see I've conquered your disapproval," he murmured.

"You haven't," she assured him. "But you're an invalid. I don't want to upset you."

"Very laudable. But I am *not* an invalid."

While he distracted her with talk, Lee had been pulling down the straps of her nightgown and began to caress her breasts. The touch of his fingers against her bare skin was agonizingly good, but Diana forced herself to seize him and protest, "No, darling..."

Lee spoke lightly, but there was a shadow behind his eyes as he asked, "Have I reached the bit you don't like?"

"Don't talk foolishness," she begged. "You know how I feel—how I love you to touch me—but I'm trying to stop things getting out of hand."

"*You're* trying! Your decision! Don't I have something to say? Maybe I *want* things to get out of hand?"

"You're not strong enough yet."

His eyes kindled. "Sooner or later we're going to have put that to the test. Diana, tell me—are you really afraid that I haven't gotten my strength back, or that I *have*?"

She looked puzzled for a moment, but then her face cleared. "You mean am I one of those women who enjoy nursing a man so that she can feel indispensable?"

"Not exactly. I mean something more than that. Hell, I wish I was better with words. I want you to stop seeing me as someone who needs your care. I want to know what happens when I throw away the crutches and stand up without you. Could you love me if I didn't need you?''

After a long moment Diana answered slowly. ''If you don't need me, you don't love me.''

And there was the bind they were in. Love thrived on opposites. True love made the lover dependent and independent, free and enslaved, strong and weak. Suddenly it seemed to Lee that he was a great fool to be trying to disentangle what philosophers since time began had been content to leave a paradox. He was here alone with a woman who touched him as no other woman had ever done. He knew that she felt the same about him. Their hearts yearned for each other as eagerly as their flesh, and there was no longer anything to keep them apart.

He said, ''I shall always love you Diana. I think I've loved you from the first moment. Wasn't it the same with you?''

''Yes,'' she said simply.

''Any other couple would long ago have passed the point we've reached.''

''But it's different for us—for you—'' She laid a careful hand on his chest.

''There's nothing different. I'm a man in love... I want to show you that love. Haven't we waited long enough? Don't you want me too?''

''You know I want you,'' she said hoarsely.

''I hope you do,'' he said, taking her into his arms again, ''because I'm not waiting any longer.''

He kissed her, but this time it felt different from before. Now he was a lover on the verge of complete fulfillment. Diana's blood raced with excitement as she felt the determined intent in his lips, his embrace. She couldn't struggle with her feelings any longer. Now she could admit to herself that she couldn't have endured it if he hadn't wanted her. He rained small kisses over her face and neck, and she sighed with luxurious pleasure as her sensitized skin glowed with response. She could feel that response extend over the length of her willing body. This was just the beginning and she would enjoy every moment of it, knowing that what was to come would be more beautiful still.

When he probed her lips she let them fall gladly apart to welcome him. As his tongue entered her mouth, she felt the tip gliding across, leaving traces of fire wherever it went. The clean smell of his body reached her, heightening her pleasure with its hint of intimacy and enfolding warmth. Her senses were more alive now than they had ever been, aching to experience him and enjoy what only he could give. More than this, her heart seemed to flower with his touch, yearning toward oneness with him.

Gently he finished taking down the straps of her nightgown, letting it slip to the floor so that she stood naked. He threw off his pajama jacket, but let her undo the trousers and glide her hands over his hips and buttocks as they were revealed. When he drew her close again, they were still reveling in the sensation of each other's nakedness. Always before they had drawn back before this point, but now they both knew there could be no drawing back from the fulfillment of love that had been their destiny since the first moment. The time for caution was past. Now they were only each other's.

Diana ran her hands over his arms and torso, but instead of the wastage of illness that she'd been so aware of before, now she felt only the wiry strength and the thought of it thrilled her. Lee took her hand

and led her back to the bed, drawing her down beside him and taking her into his arms. He kissed her deeply, tenderly, while his hands began an eager exploration of her slim body.

This was what Diana had longed for through many feverish, empty nights. Now that it was happening she was dazed with joy. She reached for him lovingly, caressing him in return. Everything about him was dear to her, and when he bent his head to lay his lips at the base of her throat she arched back, offering herself to him joyfully. His tongue moved purposefully on her soft skin, tracing whorls that flowered into patterns, spreading sweet sensation throughout her body. She hadn't known that anything could feel so ecstatic, but then, she'd never lain in the arms of a man that she loved as deeply as she loved Lee.

He cupped one full breast in his hand, then he began to tease the nipple with lips and tongue until it peaked. Diana held him to her, head thrown back, pressing herself against him in passionate eagerness, while her breathing came deep and slow. Tension mounted in her as he treated the other breast the same way, tantalizing it with soft, caressing movements until it told him what he wanted to know. Excitement spread through her body. Once she felt his leg slide between hers, she opened to him willingly.

Lee murmured her name again and again as he came into her, and she whispered his in return. The feelings that enveloped her were so powerful, so moving, that only his name could express them, his name said until eternity, their breaths mingling in the same perfect union as their bodies.

They were one as nature had meant them to be, giving and receiving love and desire in equal measure.

He asked and she answered, then she asked and received in reply a cascade of love and tenderness, passion and warmth. He moved slowly inside her, exploring her response with each thrust, loving her gently yet with an increasing power that thrilled her.

She'd come to a new place, one she'd never glimpsed before, where sensation became one with emotion, and pleasure could only exist as an aspect of love. The more she loved this man the more she wanted to please him, and the more he pleased her. With a soft gasp she drew her legs together behind his back, claiming him forever as she felt his movements become faster.

She had no thought now of control, only of ecstasy dissolving into joy. Their moment was a mutual conquest and surrender. Even the aftermath was sweet as their shudders subsided and they held each other close in reaffirmation of the wonder that had happened.

And then they lay in silence, his head on her breast, his body enclosed in her arms. As she heard the change in his breathing that meant he had fallen asleep, Diana lay staring into the darkness, outwardly calm but inwardly weeping for joy.

She tightened her arms about him and told herself that Lee was hers to cherish and keep, just as she was his in any way he wanted, and she would never let him go.

Eight

Lee came in from the garden, hot and dusty after a romp with Fang. It took some time to persuade the hound that the game was finally over, but at last he managed it and went to see if Diana had returned from a consultation with a client whose case was due as soon as the courts reopened next week. But she wasn't back yet, so he got himself a beer from the fridge.

He could hear some humming from behind the door of Diana's office and looked in curiously. Vita was there, pulling books out, dusting vigorously behind them, and pushing them back. She jumped when she saw him, then sat down, blowing out her cheeks with relief.

"I didn't mean to scare you," Lee said with a grin. "Did you think I was a ghost."

"Worse. I thought you were Di. She doesn't really like me coming in here, so I have to do the cleaning while she's out. And there's things I'm not ever sup-posed to touch.''

"Like what?'' Lee asked, intrigued.

"Like this cupboard I'm dusting now,'' Vita ad-mitted. "I give it a quick going over every so often, but I pretend I don't.''

Lee grinned. "Does Diana know?''

"Probably. It's hard to put anything across her. But as long as she doesn't actually see me she pretends and I pretend, so we get by. I always say it's pretending that makes the world go around.''

"I thought it was love that did that.''

"Well, half the time love is no more than pretend-ing,'' Vita said tartly.

"What a cynic you are,'' he chided her.

Vita snorted. "That's as may be. When I see the mess some people get themselves into by falling in love, I think a little cynicism is a good thing.''

"Nonsense,'' he declared with the assurance of a happy lover. "Look, Vita, can't I do something to help? I hate being useless. I offered to help Martin in the garden, but he refused in case Diana got mad at him.''

"Are you sure you're up to it?'' she asked guard-edly.

Lee groaned. "Not you as well. Of course I'm up to it.''

"All right. Thank you. You can hand me those books.'' She pointed to a pile on the floor.

They were large books, about the size of telephone directories. As Lee lifted them, one slipped out of his hand and landed open, revealing a succession of photographs. He picked it up and glanced at the pictures. "What's this? A family album?" he asked, intrigued.

"It looks like it," Vita said, peering over his shoulder. "Di's never shown it around. But then, she's not much of a one for telling people what's going on inside her. You have to guess."

"I should think you know her pretty well," Lee observed.

"Oh yes," Vita said calmly. "She's more transparent than she thinks she is." She gathered up her dusters. "I'm going to put the kettle on. Put that back in the cupboard when you've finished with it, won't you?"

"Sure," he said mechanically.

He went to sit in the window. A feeling of tension and excitement was rising in him as he realized he might have stumbled on one of the keys to Diana's inner self. She seemed open and candid, yet at the same time was mysterious and elusive. Sometimes he felt he understood her, and at others he knew his understanding was no more than a mirage. Here in these photos he could at least be sure of finding solid facts.

At first he thought the book had nothing to do with her at all. The pictures showed a pretty young woman with a gruff looking child who glared at the camera as if she hated it. Only after peering closely at the child's face could he be sure that this was Diana.

Her mother, for so he assumed the woman was, had been a pink-and-white doll with blond hair and wide eyes. She was always made up with model perfection, even when posing with her newborn baby. This picture was sentimentally captioned "Erica and her little angel" in small, neat handwriting.

After that the pictures seemed to have been taken at six month intervals, with the infant becoming less angelic as she grew older. The features that were strong and beautiful now had been only strong then. Diana's childhood face revealed personality and intelligence, but it was totally devoid of her mother's prettiness: a prettiness that Lee considered slightly vacuous.

The only thing the two had in common was the chin, but whereas in Diana it was resolute, in her mother it looked weakly obstinate. Erica wore soft, fluttery draperies and posed as if she saw herself as a fairy princess. Lee wondered what she'd made of the child with the high intellectual forehead and air of resolution. But of course, he realized, the answer was there in the fluffy, feminine dresses that the little girl wore so incongruously, which also must have taken such a battle to get her into. Erica had tried to turn an imp into an angel, and the resulting tension vibrated from every picture.

He went through the book to the end, then turned back to the beginning, studying each picture individually. One of them almost made him laugh out loud. Erica, in evening dress, knelt to embrace her daughter in an attitude of self-conscious mother love. Diana, her hair tortured into curls, her small wiry body encased in a frilly party frock, endured the whole business with an expression of glum resignation. Lee grinned, visualizing the child racing off to get out of the hated Sunday best after the last shot was taken. He had a feeling of knowing Diana better, which made him happy.

Just as he was about to close the book he realized that the back page had been stuck to the cover on three sides, effectively making an envelope. Gingerly he inserted his fingers inside and found another picture.

It was Diana again, but a Diana transformed. She wore jeans and a T-shirt and a blazingly happy smile. She was with a lavishly handsome man, and now Lee could see where she inherited her looks, with the exception of her chin, for her father's looks were marred by a chin that seemed curiously weak in contrast to his little daughter's. Lee wondered what this man had been like. He'd often seen that kind of boyish face in the dock. It was the face of a weakling, who would cut and run at the first sign of trouble. But his daughter seemed to adore him. He was seated, and she stood behind him with her arms about his neck, her chin on top of his head, her whole being radiating joy.

"What are you doing?"

He looked up, startled by the sound of the icy voice from the doorway. Diana was standing there in outdoor clothes, her face paler than he had ever seen it, her eyes blazing with a strange, cold light.

"I was just looking through your photos," he said. "You don't mind, do you?"

Diana came into the room and took the album from him. "Where did you get this?"

"Don't make it sound like a crime," he prevaricated, not wanting to reply truthfully and implicate Vita. "It's only a photo album. You could have shown it to me yourself."

"But I didn't. I have my reasons. All I ask is a little privacy, Lee. Is that too much?"

The bleak look in her eyes worried him, and he said gently, "If it bothers you, I'm sorry. I never meant to hurt you."

"I'm not hurt," she said quickly. "It's just that I hate to think of your looking in here without my knowing."

"Why? What difference does it make?"

"I don't know. I can't explain it." She gave an unconvincing laugh. "I must remember to lock that cupboard against Vita in future, mustn't I?"

"Why must you? Why lock yourself away from people who love you?"

"I don't. It isn't like that. It's just that parts of me are private."

"Including your parents? I shared mine with you."

"Your parents are still with you," she flashed. "It would be difficult to introduce you to mine."

"I'm sorry," he said quietly. "It's been such a long time since they—that is, I didn't realize it would still hurt you so much. I suppose I've been very clumsy, but I hate it when you hide yourself away from me. What is it you're afraid of?"

He reached out for her but she moved away. "That's a nonsensical thing to say," she snapped.

"Well, I think it's pretty nonsensical for you to act as if I were a peeping Tom just because I looked at a few pictures of you as a child."

"Behind my back." Diana knew she was making too much of it, but a demon seemed to have taken hold of her and was driving her on. She felt the same sense of intolerable invasion she'd known when Lee had interpreted her mind accurately to Clive. Instinctively she lashed out to fight the invasion off, unable to look further and see how she could be damaging the most precious relationship of her life.

"That's a bit melodramatic, isn't it?" Lee demanded. "For pity's sake, you found me looking at a family photo album not going through your purse."

"A *private* album that you were looking through without my knowledge or consent." To her dismay Diana heard herself speaking in the precise manner she often adopted to make her voice carry in court. If only something would happen to stop this, she thought desperately, but it had escalated out of her control with terrifying speed.

"All right," Lee said, raising his voice in his exasperation. "I'm sorry. I shouldn't have done it. Shall I wear sackcloth and ashes for the rest of my life, or would you prefer to have me beheaded?"

"Don't be absurd," she said, flushing at his derisive tone.

"Who's being absurd? You were talking to me like a prosecuting counsel, did you realize that? I don't want to find myself in the dock just because we're having a row, although I don't know why we're having one at all."

"Then let's stop having one," she said crisply. "Let's pretend it didn't happen."

"Fine."

It could have ended there, but Lee was left with a feeling of injustice that made him say almost immediately, "No, not fine. I don't want to leave loose ends lying around to snare us later. What's it all about Diana? Did Judge Waldman's veneer of respectability mask a guilty secret? Is there some cryptic code on the back of those pictures that reveals where he hid the body? Come on, let's have it out."

"It's all a big joke to you, isn't it?" she cried.

"When you're so totally unreasonable, yes. I committed a minor social indiscretion, not a major crime."

"All right. I admit that. It's my fault and I'm sorry I made a fuss. Now let's leave it. It's nearly time for tea and I'm hungry."

To his dismay she was smiling, appearing resolute, as if she were slamming the door on the issue. It flashed across his mind suddenly that an argument might provoke her to reveal more of herself than he'd ever discovered before. All the Fortuno family were experts in the art of creative squabbling, the kind that bound them closer together afterward. But he could see this idea was foreign to Diana. Her smile was implacable. "For pity's sake," he yelled suddenly, "call me some names. Throw the frying pan at me if you want to, but stop being so damned English and well-bred!"

"Call you names! That's your idea of rational argument, is it?"

"I don't want rational argument! Rational argument is just going to get us deeper into the mire, can't you see that? If you called me a clumsy dunderhead with no more sense than a flea, at least I'd know what you were *thinking*, and it would make a nice change from the way you talk in court."

"Well, I'm afraid I can't bring myself to throw things or hurl insults at you, so let's leave it there, shall we?" she said, tight-lipped.

"Yes, by all means, let's leave it there. Whatever we do, don't let's try to sort out what's wrong between us. You'll do anything rather than admit your problems, won't you?"

"Lee," she said with strained patience, "apart from being harassed by you, trying to make me admit to problems I don't have, I have no problems. All right?"

"All right, all right," he said placatingly, knowing he'd lost.

Everyone was very cheerful at supper. Vita had tried a new recipe to universal applause. Martin's newly harvested vegetables were pronounced a big success. Clive started quoting Latin, which according to Vita, meant that he'd fallen in love "yet again," which was confirmed by Clive's embarrassment. But behind the laughter the atmosphere was fraught. Diana and Lee seemed unable to look at each other, while the other three frequently exchanged puzzled glances.

Later that evening Diana came and knocked on Lee's door. When he saw her standing there, pale and apprehensive, his heart went out to her and he opened his arms. She went into them, finding the refuge she longed for. "I'm sorry I was such a beast," she muttered against his shoulder.

"You weren't. It was my fault. I shouldn't have looked into your private album, but I didn't realize it mattered that much." He kissed her tenderly, assailed by the feeling of unhappiness that emanated from her. "Why does it matter so much?" he whispered. "Can't you tell me?"

"I guess I'm just a bit crazy," she sighed.

His heart sank again as he recognized a put off answer. While he was trying to decide whether to press the matter, she drew away from him. Taking a step back, she took something from a little table in the hall. It was the album. "I brought it to show you," she said. "Not that I relish the sight of myself as I was then. Wasn't I hideous?"

"You weren't as beautiful as you are now," he conceded, drawing her into the room. He sat on the bed and began to turn the pages. When he came to the end he slid his fingers unobtrusively into the lining pocket. As he had half feared, it was empty. He didn't allow his disappointment to show, but continued talking. "But one thing hasn't changed. You were an awkward little cuss even then. It's there in your face."

"And I still am," she teased, sitting beside him.

"If anything, worse. You're a real shrew." They laughed together, but they both knew it was all wrong. The moment had passed, and this attempt to retrieve it was doomed to failure. "Your mother was very pretty," he said, making a valiant effort.

"Yes, she used to be a model. I never felt I could live up to her." Diana laughed awkwardly. "Pink and white just isn't my style."

"That's true. But I like your style better."

Diana looked over her shoulder at the bed. "What are you doing?"

"Starting to pack. I've stayed here too long. I'm not an invalid anymore. I was going to tell you tomorrow."

"Don't rush things," she said quickly. "You'll dash back to work before you're ready—"

"They won't let me work until the police doctor has passed me fit, so don't worry." He squeezed her hand. "You can't look after me forever," he added quietly.

"Are you sure that's the only reason?"

"I'm not going because we had a row, silly," he chided her. "What an ungrateful wretch you must think me."

But it wasn't as simple as that. He knew he'd indulged himself disgracefully by lingering in her sweet company. It was only today that a chill breeze had blown and told him that for a while he must set a little distance between them.

Diana slowed her car as Lee's apartment building came in sight. His windows were at the back, so she couldn't see if he was home, and now that she was here her stomach was churning with unaccustomed nerves.

Lee had been gone for four days. He'd called her the first evening to thank her again for her care of him. She'd found herself examining every nuance of that call, every slight shading of his voice, trying to read into it what her heart needed to know, that he was as desolate without her as she already was without him. Although his manner had been friendly he hadn't mentioned another meeting. Something had gone subtly wrong between them, and she was tormented by an unaccustomed feeling of helplessness. Whatever she did might make things worse.

She'd told herself to be patient but she yearned for him, lying awake each night, hearing again the sound of his beloved voice, seeing his face smiling with warmth and tenderness. Had it only been her imagination that he had looked at her with love?

After four days she'd remembered the spare key to his apartment that was still in her possession and decided it was her duty to restore it to him personally. Trusting it to the post would be enormously risky. She didn't call him first, but drove straight over that evening. Now she was here, and she was afraid. The sight of his face when he first saw her would confirm her hopes or her worst fears.

But there was no reply when she rang his bell. After hesitating for a long while she opened the front door, timidly looking inside. The light was fading fast and the apartment was in semidarkness. She stepped inside tentatively, feeling like a trespasser in the silence.

It would have been easy to leave the key on the kitchen table, with a brief note, which is what she'd begun to do, but then decided against it. He'd be back soon and he surely wouldn't mind finding her here. She sat down to wait.

After an hour she told herself that he must be working. A policeman's hours were unpredictable. She should go. But her heart rebelled against leaving without seeing him. She gave a wry smile at herself, knowing that the old, strong-minded Diana would have been too proud to let a man suspect that she ached to see him just once more. But that Diana didn't seem to exist anymore. In her place was this rawly vulnerable woman with unpredictable emotions. Never before had she felt about any other man as she felt about Lee. Her decision was made. She'd wait just a few more minutes, then act firmly. Wearily she closed her eyes.

She awoke to find the room beginning to fill with the gray light of dawn. When she was able to focus in on the clock it was showing five. She leaped up in a panic, her cheeks burning. Lee hadn't been home all night. Dear God, he mustn't arrive and find her now!

Diana left the key with a note on the table, then she hurried out. To her relief there was no one about as she went down to her car. She tried to keep her thoughts blank as she drove home. Lee had been working, of course. She wouldn't even let herself think about the other reason why he might have chosen to spend the night away from home. And yet it seemed to her that the world was bathed in a bleak gray light that had nothing to do with the dawn.

Nine

As she approached her home Diana hoped her friends had gone to bed. In her present state she didn't feel she could endure questions. But as she drew up, the garage door began to rise. That meant one of them was sitting up for her. She could make out a light deep within the house.

As she got out of the car, Martin appeared in the door that connected the garage to the house. "You'd better get inside, quick," he said.

Wondering what could have happened she hurried past him. And then she stopped, trying to take in the incredible sight of Lee standing in the hall, his face pale, dark smudges under his eyes. "Where the hell have you been until this hour?" he demanded hoarsely.

She walked toward him in a dream. "Where have *I*—? How long have you been here?"

"All night. Vita said she was expecting you hours ago. I've been going out of my mind worrying about you. I was just about to start calling the hospitals. Diana, *where have you been?*"

She began to laugh, less from mirth than from relief and joy.The intensity of her feelings made her light-headed. She shook helplessly with laughter while Vita, Martin, and Lee gathered around her anxiously and Clive looked down over the bannisters.

"Diana," Lee said, taking her shoulders, "what is it? What's happened? Have you been in an accident?"

She shook her head, unable to speak right away. The words finally came. "It's all right," she said. "I'm not crazy, I'm not drunk. I'm just so happy."

Lee drew her against him, patting her shoulder cautiously. "Sure you are," he said soothingly. "Let's get settled and you can tell me all about it." He was removing her coat as he talked. Martin took it, leaving him free to lead her into the book room. He settled her onto the sofa, then poured her a drink, all the while watching her cautiously.

Diana wished she knew a way to prolong this glorious moment. Lee had been here all night, waiting for her, worried and scared, just as she had been. The thought sent her off again.

"At this point I'm supposed to calm you down by tossing the contents of this glass over you," he observed, "but it would be a waste of good wine, so I won't. The suspense is killing me. Darling, where have you been?"

"You won't believe me."

"Try me."

"I've been at your apartment."

"At my—? All this time?"

"I fell asleep."

"Are you telling me," he demanded in outrage, "that while I've been sitting here waiting for you, you've been sitting there waiting for me?"

She nodded, her eyes bright. Lee struggled to control his face, then abandoned the attempt and gave a shout of laughter, which he smothered by burying his face against her. "I went to return your key," Diana continued, putting her arms around him and holding him tight. "I let myself in to wait, when you didn't come I thought—that is, I wondered—"

"I know what you were wondering. I was wondering the same myself." Suddenly the laughter faded from his eyes and he spoke quietly. "But I couldn't really believe you'd forget me so soon. We have something better than that."

"Yes," she said softly. "It's just that after the way you went away I wasn't sure what we had."

"I can't remember what I was thinking. I know I was worried about something, but tonight when you didn't come home, I thought I'd lost you—that was when the nightmare really started. Nothing else was important."

"For me too."

He put his arms around her and she went into them gladly, her face upturned, seeking his lips on hers. The feel of them was inexpressibly sweet.

"We must never lose each other again," he said huskily. "I came here tonight to ask you to marry me. Say you will."

"Yes," she said at once. "I don't know what I'd do if you didn't want me. I love you so much."

"I was afraid I'd never hear you say that again."

"I'll say it every day for the rest of our lives," she said against his lips. "I'll say it until you're tired of hearing it."

"That'll be never," he murmured.

Diana felt as though her life had started. Nothing that had happened before she knew this man was of any importance. The misery of the past few days vanished as though it had never been.

Lee took her hand and rose to his feet, drawing her from the room then up the stairs. On the landing he hesitated, then let her lead him the rest of the way to her room.

Once inside he seized her hungrily in his arms, kissing her with fierce intent, letting her know with every movement how desperately he'd longed for her. Diana responded equally, feeling her heart swell with joy at being in his arms again, the only place she ever wanted to be.

They began to undress each other feverishly. A moment ago Diana had been worn out. Now new life flowed through her veins as she thought of lying naked in his arms and showing him what he was to her. She'd forced herself to repress her feelings, but they were ready to burst forth in an explosion of love and passion. She stripped away his shirt, then his trousers, eagerly seeking the body she remembered could give her such marvelous sensations with its power and tenderness.

She felt her blouse pulled from her, then her bra, then his hand was on her breast, teasing her with the skillful caresses he knew she loved. She leaned against him, kissing him urgently in return, exploring him with her hands. "Everything's still just as you left it," he murmured in her ear, sounding amused. "Still yours, still wanting you."

As he spoke he picked her up and took her to the bed. Laying her there, he began to work on the fastening of her skirt. At the same moment she reached for the waistband of his underpants, and their hands collided. They laughed at their own impatience and redoubled their efforts.

But then the laughter died and their eyes met in silence. They were awed by how close they'd come to losing each other and swept by the passionate relief of being together again. Lee put up a gentle hand and touched her face, stroking her cheeks with reverent fingers, then letting his fingertips drift across her mouth. Diana shivered at that touch, feeling a thousand tremors go through her.

He laid his lips on hers and began to move them slowly, relishing the recovery of what he treasured. Her mouth was sweet wine after the dreary abstinence of their separation. He drank deeply, feeling his heart refreshed.

Diana parted her lips to him, eager to entice him in where she could offer up the gifts he loved. His tongue was a teasing challenge that she met gladly. Excitement spread through her as he explored her mouth, rediscovering its dark warmth. She caressed him with feverish hands, knowing now that she had him back she must keep him, because he was everything to her. She sought out the lean length of his back, reveling in the feel of the muscles rippling under the smooth skin. Her nostrils were full of the musky odor of his arousal that spoke directly to her senses and thrilled her unbearably.

Lee was lavishing kisses all over her face, murmuring, "We must never let it happen again...I can't bear to be apart from you ... promise me ..."

"I promise," she said huskily, "I'll never let you go."

"Love me—always."

"Always," she murmured, speaking breathlessly through the mounting sensation that constricted her throat.

His kisses had drifted to the place below her ear, making her sigh with delight, then lower to the base of her throat. She arched against him, rejoicing in the power he had to inflame her senses. Her body was tuned to his loving, thrumming with sweet harmonies and wild songs.

His tongue was tracing patterns on her creamy skin, gliding down until it could curl about one rosy nipple already peaked in readiness. Diana let out a long sigh of aching delight and frustration as he began to torment it softly. "Lee..." she whispered pleadingly.

"I've dreamed of loving you again," he murmured, "and now that I have you I'm going to savor you slowly. You're too perfect to rush."

She could feel his manhood, hard and throbbing against her thigh. He wanted her as badly as she wanted him, but he was a man of great patience. It was Diana, normally so controlled, who found this restraint unendurable. She wanted what only Lee could give her, release from the bonds that constrained her everyday self, freedom to be herself, her true self, the self that nature had meant her to be before pain and betrayal had taken their toll.

He was kissing her everywhere, in the hollow of her waist, over the roundness of her hips to the soft, sensitive skin of her inner thighs. She was burning to take him, to make him hers once more in the union that completed them both. She clasped him with yearning hands and he read her message, yielding at last to his own passion and hers, letting her draw him between her legs.

From now on it was she who took the lead, urging him on with words and movements, making love to him with all of her. As he entered her she met him halfway, enclosing him deeply within her body as she already enclosed him within her heart. For her the joy of their mating was more than its physical pleasure, it was the sum total of everything that had happened between them, and looking up into his eyes she saw that it was the same with him. Their shared moment was a reaffirmation of love and commitment, and they ended it still clasped in each other's arms as ecstasy ebbed away and blissful content took its place.

They slept for a while, limbs entwined, then awoke and loved again. Diana would have liked to doze off once more beside him, but it was morning and she could hear Vita making noises in the kitchen. She knew her happiness couldn't be complete until her mind was eased of one problem. "Lee, about where we're going to live—" she began.

He forestalled her. "We shall live here, naturally. We couldn't possibly fit Vita and Martin in my little apartment. Not to mention Fang and Suki and John Wayne."

She sighed happily. "I was afraid you might not understand."

"I think I understand you pretty well," he said tenderly. "I know you're not going to abandon your protégés, even for me."

"I couldn't be happy if I did."

"That's what I thought. The only stipulation I make is that I pay my half of the expenses, bills, mortgage etc."

"There's no mortgage. The house was paid for outright ages ago."

"So, let them say I'm a kept man," Lee said light-heartedly. "What do I care?"

There was a rap on the bedroom door. "Don't worry. I'm not coming in," Vita called. "I've left your tea on the table out here."

Lee smothered his mirth against Diana's breasts. "I think Vita learned tact from your mother," she said, caressing his hair.

She got up and threw on a robe to look out into the corridor. The tray she brought in contained not only tea, but a plate of freshly baked ginger biscuits. Lee fell on them with delight. "I have no intention of being deprived of Vita's ginger biscuits," he said with his mouth full. "I suspect you're a terrible cook." Diana shook her head. "You're *not* a terrible cook?"

"I don't know. I've never tried," she told him mischievously.

Lee eyed her in horrified fascination. "You can't cook *anything*?"

She shook her head. "Not a thing. I've always resisted learning. I hate cooking. Your mother would have a fit, wouldn't she?"

"She would if it wasn't you. But my mother adores you and considers you on a different plane to other women." He hastily nabbed the last biscuit.

"What will she say when she knows we're going to get married?" Diana asked.

"She'll ask what took me so long. Darling, my mother has known we were going to get married ever since she met you. Let's call her now, shall we?"

Diana shook her head. "Afterward," she said, going to lock the bedroom door.

"Afterward?"

"Yes." Diana let her robe fall to the floor and came to slide her arms about his neck. "Afterward."

Ten

The clerk of the court intoned. "Do you find the prisoner, Frank Morris, guilty or not guilty?"

The foreman of the jury cleared his throat nervously. "Guilty," he said.

Five minutes later Morris was on his way to start a two-year sentence, and those who had been connected with his case were gathering their things to leave the court. His defense counsel, a grizzled elderly man called Jeremy Frane, signaled to Lee to wait for him outside.

He emerged into the lobby of the Old Bailey a few minutes later and hailed Lee. "It's far too long since we had a drink," he said in a voice that had grown hoarse from too much whisky, too many cigars, and too many speeches in court. He looked what he was, an embattled old war-horse, whom Lee was very fond of.

"Bad luck," he said now, sympathetically.

Frane shrugged. "You win some, you lose some. My only hope of winning this one was to make you collapse in the witness box, and since you wouldn't oblige, what could I do?"

"You gave me a hard time," Lee said truthfully.

"All in the day's work. No offense, I hope."

"None taken."

They entered a pub where the food was good and the ale tasted like the real thing. "Morris was as guilty as hell," Lee observed. "Seeing how often you've represented him and his family in the past, that can't come as much of a surprise to you."

"Yes, I don't know how I'd have paid for the odd bottle of claret if the Morrises had been luckier in their encounters with the law. Well, I shall soon be out of it."

"Don't tell me you're thinking of retiring?"

"More than thinking of it. I'm definitely taking the plunge. I've been at the bar for forty years, and that's quite long enough for a man who wants to keep his sanity."

"I wouldn't have thought you were that old," Lee said, telling a kind lie, for Frane looked his age or more.

"I started when Horace Waldman had just been appointed a judge. It was my ill luck to get him on my very first case. Lord, but that man was a devil. Full of deadly politeness that stabbed you to the heart. I always say he cut his teeth on me. He filed them to murderous weapons on later victims, but he first cut them on me." He assumed a thin, sarcastic voice. "'Take your time, Mr. Frane. The law of this land evolved over a thousand years. It can wait a little longer for you to be ready.' And there I was, as nervous as a cat, dropping papers all over the place.

"I was defending a man called Billings on a theft charge. The prosecution case was weak and I knew I ought to win. Waldman knew it too. He kept interrupting me to tell me what I ought to have asked, and somehow I stumbled through it, wishing I were dead. He sat up there, completely inscrutable, and I waited for him to tear me to shreds in his summing up. But he summed up in my favor. I could hardly believe my ears. Not that he was praising me. He practically told the jury that they should acquit Billings because the poor devil hadn't been properly defended. And they did.

"Waldman was like that. Fair to the last thousandth of an ounce, but he didn't give his thoughts away and he couldn't bring himself to be kind. A real hard old flint. I never could understand how he came to give a home to that little granddaughter of his."

"I suppose he felt it was his duty when her parents died," Lee remarked.

Frane looked at him in astonishment. "Her parents didn't die."

"Of course they did. There was nowhere else for her to go."

"That's as may be, but they're not dead. They divorced. It was a messy divorce too. The mother ran off with a younger man, and the father raked up every bit of mud he could find in court because he was trying to save himself alimony. Nasty business."

A strange feeling was taking hold of Lee. It was composed equally of incredulity and a kind of fear. He wasn't quite sure why he should be afraid. It was obvious that there had been some mistake, but he wished his heart would stop beating so hard. The last time it had thumped like this was when he'd stared down the barrel of a gun a few months ago and known that the next few seconds would decide his fate. "A divorce wouldn't explain why Diana went to live with her grandfather," he said in a voice that didn't sound like his own.

"But my dear fellow, neither of them wanted her. Her mother was a bit of a fly-by-night. Probably still is. Empty-headed. Never thought of anything except buying expensive clothes and having a good time. She's living in Majorca now. A friend of mine saw her there last year with a new man in tow. Apparently they get younger and younger. He said she seemed very 'well preserved.'

"Her father lives up north somewhere, owns a couple of rather tacky nightclubs. They don't make any money, but they provide him with an endless succession of scantily clad females, which seems to be all he asks of life. The poor little mite was probably better off without them. Still, it was a bit thick, just dumping her, don't you think?"

"Yes," Lee said, staring into space, "I do."

Frane emptied his glass. "Whatever made you think they were dead?"

It was a casual question, and Lee wondered what would happen if he came out with what was in his head: *"I thought they were dead because Diana told me they were. I've now realized that the dream of warmth and love that seemed to enfold me was only an illusion; that the woman I adore has been hiding her secret self from me all this time."*

But he was too proud to let Frane suspect that he, who loved Diana, had been left ignorant of something so important to her.

"Shall we have the steak and kidney pie?" Frane was musing. "It's very good here."

"I'm sorry, I can't stay," Lee said. "I have to rush away."

"But I thought you said you were free this evening?"

"Yes, but—I've just remembered something I have to do. Sorry, Frane. Let's make it another time."

He was almost out of the door as he spoke. He knew he had to get into the cool fresh air, had to be alone. His head felt as if it might explode.

He began to walk mechanically, not looking where he was going. Somehow he found himself in the park. His legs ached as if he'd walked for miles. He found a seat by the lake and sat staring at the ducks. But he couldn't see them. He was seeing something else, a child of ten, trying to come to terms with the fact that neither of her parents wanted her. His vivid imagination showed him the little girl's grief and bewilderment, and his heart ached for her. He wanted to reach back through time and comfort that unhappy child.

But she didn't want his comfort. Diana had shared with him moments of happiness and laughter, and done it so thoroughly that he'd thought he'd finally possessed her whole self. All the time he'd had only the surface, because she had been shutting him out from the grief of her life. The pain of that discovery made it hard to breathe.

Gradually pain turned to bitterness and anger as he reflected what a fool she'd made of him. He rose and began to walk again until he returned to where he'd parked his car. He started the engine with no clear idea of where he was going. He knew he shouldn't see Diana while he was in this mood, that if he did it would lead to a quarrel in which they would both say unforgivable things. But he found himself taking the turn that led to her home.

He let himself in and went straight through to her study. She looked up and smiled, but the smile faded when she saw his pale face. "What is it, Lee? Has something terrible happened?"

"I'm not sure." He took a deep breath. "Diana, when did your parents die?"

Her face grew as pale as his. "What did you say?"

"They both died before you were ten, didn't they? Were you there when it happened? Did you attend their funerals? Where are they buried?"

In the silence he saw her face close against him. He hadn't known until then how much he'd hoped to find that it had been a mistake. But instead of bewilderment, there was only a hard look in her eyes, and his heart seemed to shrivel.

"What have you done?" she whispered.

"What have I done? I've loved and trusted you."

"It was love and trust, was it, that made you ask about me behind my back? *I* trusted *you*."

"Not enough to tell me the truth, evidently," Lee said coldly.

"Enough to take it for granted that you wouldn't act like a policeman with a suspect whose story had to be checked," she flashed.

He clenched his hands against the pain her words gave him. "I didn't check up on you," he said through gritted teeth. "I found out by accident."

"How?"

"Someone told me over a beer. It doesn't matter who. It could have been anyone. There are plenty of lawyers around who knew your grandfather. You should have thought of that before you lied to me."

"Oh, God!" Diana said in despair. She turned away from him, trying to subdue the turmoil in her heart. The thought of being common gossip revolted her.

Lee took a step toward her, moved by a gentler impulse. He could see her pain, and it tore at him. If they could only stop hurting each other, if she would only let him put his arms about her and offer her all the comfort his loving heart could give. "Why must you keep things to yourself?" he asked quietly.

"It seems to make no difference," she said with soft bitterness. "The police have their methods of finding out haven't they?"

"I've already told you it wasn't like that," he said angrily. "It was an accident. What matters is what it's done to us. What do you think it was like discovering that you'd kept something so vital from me? I wanted to bang my head against the wall. I wanted it not to be true."

"Why?" she demanded sharply. "What does it matter? Why do you make so much of it? You talk of trust. Have I betrayed that trust? Have I played you false with any other man?"

"In a way I think you have played me false. Not with another man, but by letting me believe something that wasn't true."

"That my parents were dead?" she cried incredulously. "Why does it matter so much?"

"Because I thought you'd allowed me into your heart when all the time I'd only gotten past an outer door." Bitterness infused his voice. "You still keep the inner one bolted and barred, but you made damned sure I never suspected that."

"I left out one small detail about my life," she said in a careful voice that showed she, too, had seen the dangerous path they were treading. "Why should it matter so much? Have you told me everything about your life?"

"I've told you the important things. Your parents were two selfish people who rejected you for their own convenience. *One small detail?* It's the source of everything that matters about you, and you know it."

For Diana it was as though the sky had fallen in on her. She wanted to put her hands over her ears to shut out the things Lee was saying. Secrets she couldn't bear to think about even in the privacy of her own head had been yanked into the daylight. She felt threatened and apprehensive, and it was Lee who had done this to her.

Suddenly he looked like an enemy. When he said her parents' betrayal was the root of everything, she felt something snap inside her. "That's not true," she cried desperately. "It's the past. It's over. I'm what my grandfather made me and what I made myself. My parents aren't part of me anymore."

"You can't really believe that. No child could come through such an experience without being affected. The very fact that you pretend they're dead shows how much they count."

"To me they *are* dead, and it's nobody's business but mine."

"That story will do for strangers, but not for me. Can't you understand that I want to share everything with you, including what you've suffered? I don't just want the good parts, I want everything, because that's the only kind of relationship that means anything to me. If you can't tell me what hurts you, what are we? What's the point of loving each other? Or don't we love each other? Have I been fooling myself about that, too, all this time? Has everything I thought was between us been nothing but an illusion?"

"Perhaps it has," she cried raggedly. "I certainly don't know you anymore."

"And you don't want what I have to offer, do you?" he asked in a strange voice. "Not just love, but comfort too. If I was wounded I'd have limped any distance to find you and have you bind it up for me, because no hands but yours would do. But if you were wounded you'd turn away from me."

She turned away from him now, arms crossed over her chest as if to keep him out, silently beating off his invasion. She knew it was an invasion of love and potential understanding. There was still time to stop this. She could hold out her arms to him and he would come to her. Except that she couldn't. The stern self-control of years refused to crumble. "I can't help it," she said desperately. "Looking after myself is what I'm used to. I don't know how to change."

"Then God help you," he whispered. "Do you know how lonely you're going to be?"

From the kitchen came the distant sound of Vita's and Martin's voices raised in friendly bickering. Diana gave a hard laugh. "Why should I be lonely? This house is never empty."

"Oh yes, your lame dogs," he said bitterly. "There's always been something about your passion for them that worried me, and now I know what it is. It's just another barrier to hide behind, isn't it? It's the only kind of relationship where you feel comfortable, because it puts you in control. You can give but you don't know how to take, because taking means letting people see where you're vulnerable, and you don't trust anyone enough to do that—not even me. I can't live with a woman who hides herself from me.''

She knew she was losing him, and something in her screamed at the thought. But she'd become immobile. The words of passionate love and longing wouldn't come out even if it meant the end of her life. She wanted to cry "Stay with me. I need you." But her throat was tight and hard, blocking all speech.

"I can't love part of you, Diana," Lee said sadly. "It has to be all or nothing."

She stared bleakly into space. "Let it be nothing, then," she said.

Lee stopped at the entrance to Wendle House. He was making this visit in his first available off-duty hour, even though he hadn't been able to plan for a moment when Diana would or wouldn't be there. However, from what he gathered, she was out. It had rained that day, but now the rain had stopped, giving way to a beautiful late summer sunset. There were no tire marks on the wet paving stones leading to the garage door.

It was a week since they had parted, a week during which he'd been through all stages of misery and disbelief until he'd come back to where he'd started. His heart ached to see her again, but he hadn't returned. She must come to him. He told himself this wasn't pride, merely an acknowledgement of reality. It was Diana's emotional stubbornness that created the barrier between them and only she could break it down.

He was here now to retrieve some of his possessions that were still in the house. He walked around the side to the kitchen window, through which he could see Vita and Martin. He tapped on the window and Vita looked up. She gave a brief smile and let him in by the back door. "I was just making some coffee," she said. "Di's out, I'm afraid."

"Good. I doubt if she'd want to see me," Lee said.

"Then it's a pity you came," Martin informed him shortly. "I said you were riffraff the night she brought you here, and riffraff is what you turned out to be."

"I just came to collect some of my clothes I left behind," Lee said.

"Then you'd better get them and be off," Martin said sourly.

Lee grimaced and left them to go to his old room. A wave of memories hit him as he opened the door. This was where Diana had cared for him and where they'd learned to love each other. Now everything was quiet, even chilly. He emptied the contents of the wardrobe into his bag as quickly as possible, then returned to the kitchen.

Vita pointed to a mug of coffee that she'd set on the table. "You're quite safe," she said. "Di won't be back until late."

"Why should she want to see him anyway?" Martin growled.

"Hush you, you old fool," Vita adjured him. To Lee she said, "Ignore him. He's just very cut up over the way it turned out. We all are."

"Me too," Lee said quietly. "I never wanted it to end like this."

"If you ask me, the two of you need your heads knocked together," Vita declared with the bluntness of true friendship.

"*He* needs his head knocked together," Martin growled illogically.

Lee grinned wryly. "If I thought it would do any good, I'd volunteer for it as a joint venture. But she's so stubborn I'm afraid I'd only end up with a dented head."

"Hrmph!" Vita said. "So *she's* stubborn, is she?"

Clive came in from the garden, carrying an armful of freshly cut roses. He greeted Lee with a nod and held out the flowers for Vita to inspect. "I just got them before the light faded," he said. "What do you think of them?"

Vita sniffed the blooms appreciatively. "They'll do. Put them in that vase over there for now, and I'll arrange them in Diana's room later."

"Not that she'll notice," Martin said. "Her mind's taken up with just one thing these days." His baleful glance at Lee made it clear whom he blamed.

"So I've been cast as the villain, have I?" Lee said, feeling ruffled. "I'm not pretending it's all Diana's fault, but I'll be damned if I can see what I could have done that was different."

"You could have made up with her," Vita said.

"How can I when *she* broke with *me*?"

"You didn't have to let her break with you, did you?" Vita said patiently, as if explaining to an idiot. "You're the one who's supposed to have his head screwed on right."

"I'd like to knock it off for him," Martin supplied darkly.

"If you can't say anything more useful than that, just pipe down," Vita ordered him tartly. "We won't get anywhere by calling names."

"Oh, that's nice," Martin said, outraged. "What about the way Di's gone around this week, looking like death warmed over? You've seen her face when she picks up the phone and it ain't him. And I'm not supposed to call him names! I know a few I'd like to call him."

"Vita's right, it won't do any good," Clive put in. "Put your horsewhip away, Martin. Lee's got a point of view as well."

"Thank you," Lee said ironically.

"Not that I think you were very smart," Clive added. "You should have expected something like this. You knew what Di was like."

"It seems I didn't," Lee said coolly.

"Then where were your eyes?" Vita demanded. "I warned you how private she could be."

"But it never seemed that she had trouble showing her emotions," Lee protested. "She often told me that she loved me."

"Even that's not like her," Vita said. "She opened up with you as I've never seen her do with anyone else." She sighed. "We had such high hopes that you might be the one she needed."

"She doesn't need anybody," Lee said bitterly. "And she'd be the first to say so."

"Of course she would," Vita responded, "but that doesn't mean you have to believe it. With your background you could have been just the man to understand her."

"Well, I don't understand a woman who shuts me out when it matters."

"But that's her way of coping. I expect you've got a few funny ways of coping too. We all have. Martin tells tall stories. Clive's a student so he boozes. You'd think his legs were hollow to watch him put it away, sometimes."

"What about you, Vita. What's your way?" Lee asked.

Vita sighed nostalgically. "I used to enjoy heaving bricks through store windows. There was something about watching plate-glass disintegrate that set me up better than a tot of whisky."

"Used to?" he queried.

"I don't need to now. I'm all right, thanks to Di."

"How do *you* cope?" Clive asked, watching Lee.

"In various ways," Lee said hastily, aware of a few minor indiscretions that had mercifully never reached the ears of his superiors. "Aren't we getting off the subject?"

"Well, it is the subject, isn't it?" Clive persisted. "Everyone has their peculiarities, and you should have tried to understand about Di's."

"You had no right to tell her that she only helps people to keep them at arm's length," Martin accused.

"That isn't exactly what I said," Lee protested.

"It's as near as dammit!" Martin growled. "Shall I tell you something, Mr. Clever Policeman? Vita and me don't care why Di took us in. Clive's got a future, but we'd have ended our days being spoon-fed in institutions. Arm's length? I'll live at the top of the Eiffel Tower if that's what suits Di, just as long as I don't have to listen to that daughter-in-law of mine telling everyone I've got a screw loose.

"What made you go into the police? Did it all for the good of your fellow citizens, did you? Don't make me laugh. You wanted excitement, and a little bit of power. Nobody's motives are perfect."

Lee looked at him ruefully, unable to remember when he'd last been so comprehensively attacked. "Well, I guess that's telling me," he said at last. He sipped his coffee to give himself time to think before saying, "However inhibited she may be with me, Diana doesn't seem to have had any trouble telling you everything."

Vita turned her eyes to heaven. "Give me patience with him, Lord!" she begged satirically. To Lee she said, "You don't really think she told us, do you?"

"Then how do you know?"

"We were listening."

"Of course. I should have thought of that."

"How can we look after her if we don't know what's going on?" Vita asked unanswerably. "And how are we to know if we don't eavesdrop? She don't tell us anything, and we don't dare ask. In the old days, when she just had little troubles, we sometimes tried to encourage her to talk. But it just seemed to make everything worse, so now we don't. It breaks my heart to see her forcing herself to smile when all I want to do is put my arms around her and tell her to cry."

"I'm glad she's got you," Lee said. "I'm beginning to realize how much you really do take care of her."

"Someone's got to," Martin said, "or she'd be alone. Look at this huge house. She won't sell it because of her grandfather's memory. He was the only person who wanted her. But it's much too big. How would she manage if we weren't here?"

"You don't know how hard we work to save her from spongers," Vita added with no sense of irony.

"What did you mean, a moment ago, when you said, 'with my background'?" Lee asked.

"I meant your family. You've had all the advantages she hasn't," Vita said quietly.

"Yes, I guess you're right." He thought for a moment. "Perhaps I'd better go now."

"What are you going to do?" Martin asked.

"I'm going to do a lot of thinking. But I need time and space to do it in, so I'd rather you didn't tell Diana I was here."

The others nodded. He took his bag, then hurried to where he'd left his car, anxious that Diana shouldn't see him before he was ready. He drove around for a while before going home to lie on his bed, staring into the darkness.

But despite all this evidence of mental activity he knew that the decision had already been made for him. As soon as Vita had said, "You've had all the advantages she hasn't," things had fallen into place. He was going back to Diana, to beg her to try again. Their love might never be easy, but together they could discover the seam of pure gold on which it was based. He just needed to get his thoughts in order first.

Understanding. He remembered how they'd used that word again and again, reproaching him for his failure to give her as much as she needed. Now he began to be ashamed of how little he'd tried. He'd accused her of being too proud to admit she was vulnerable, but that very pride was her real vulnerability and it had been staring him in the face.

Vita had said, "She opened up with you as I've never seen her do with anyone else." There was the clue, if he'd had eyes to see it. She'd chosen him because she'd sensed he was the man whose love could break down her barriers. And he'd failed her. He'd dreamed of a home that was as warm and loving as the one he'd grown up in, forgetting that his home with Diana would be what he, as well as she, would make of it.

Suddenly he wanted her desperately. He had to call her now and ask her forgiveness, tell her they'd find a way to make it work between them. Snapping on the light he reached out for the telephone, but then he stopped as he saw the clock.

It was four in the morning. Where had the time gone? He balked at the thought of attempting this tricky conversation with a woman who'd just been dragged from sleep. Everything had to be perfect.

He groaned as he remembered that next day he had a court appearance. It would have to be the evening. He began counting the hours until he could see her, hours that seemed to stretch out into infinity.

Eleven

Diana arrived at work to find a message on her desk saying that Reginald Grant, the chief partner, wanted to see her urgently. She put her head around his door and he waved her in. Reginald was a large man of nearly sixty, whose white hair and air of benevolent innocence concealed a shrewdly cynical brain. "What a relief to see you!" he said. "I've got a crisis and you're my only hope. You're free today, aren't you?"

"Yes."

"Thank heavens. George has gone down with the flu, and he's due in court this morning on the Langley case. Be a dear and take it over."

"This morning? That's not giving me much time to do it justice, Reggie. Especially as it's George."

"What's that supposed to mean?"

"You know what it means. George is a disorganized mess who doesn't bother to write down half the things he ought to. Taking over any of his cases is a nightmare. I'll have to ask for an adjournment.''

"Apparently the client doesn't want to. There've already been two adjournments for various reasons, and he wants to get it over with. He's sure he's going to win, and he wants his passport back so that he can go on holiday.''

"As confident as that? Let's hope he's right.''

"Luckily it's quite straightforward. The police are prosecuting Alfred Langley for mugging a man on a train. The victim can't identify him with any certainty, and there were no witnesses.''

"Then why was he ever charged?''

Reggie sighed as though mourning human stupidity. "He was unwise enough to confess. But that's the only evidence against him. This man claims the police bullied him into admitting something he hadn't done. You've destroyed quite a few of those confessions in the past. This one should be simple.''

"Who was the arresting officer?''

Reggie glanced at the papers. "Detective Inspector Fredericks. An old adversary of yours.''

"Yes, I know how he gets his confessions,'' Diana said grimly. "That makes it easier to believe Langley's innocent. I'll do it, Reggie.''

As she reached the door he said, "You're not going down with the flu as well, I hope.''

"No. Why?''

"You look terrible. In fact you've looked terrible for the past week, but you're even worse this morning.''

"Nonsense,'' she said firmly. "I'm perfectly well.''

"Nothing wrong, is there, Diana?''

Diana managed a laugh. "Nothing except that I work in a madhouse. That's what you told me this place was on the day I came for my interview, remember?"

"Yes, I said that only the stoutest hearts could stick it out, and your heart is as stout as any. In fact I've always admired you for the way you didn't let things get on top of you."

"Well, there you are, then. Coolness under fire is my stock-in-trade," she said lightly.

"Are you sure the fire hasn't become heavier recently?"

"Perfectly sure." She gave him a cheerful smile. "I promise you all's right with my little world, Reggie."

"Well, if you say so. Best of luck with the case."

Diana just managed to keep her mask in place until she was out of the building. She hadn't slept all night and now she was tense and nervous, and everything was an effort.

The week since she'd sent Lee away had devastated her. She'd jumped whenever the phone rang, certain that it was him. But it never was, and at last she realized that he'd taken her dismissal as final. It was over between them. She'd told him that she didn't want his love. Now it seemed he no longer wanted to love her.

At home she'd maintained a bright front, confident she'd fooled her companions. Occasionally she felt a faint trace of resentment at how easily they were fooled. She'd been their friend, but now that she was unhappy they seemed indifferent. Not one of them had reached out a hand to comfort her, which hurt more than she'd ever thought it could. It was a relief to know that she'd kept her feelings private, but somehow that seemed less important than it once had.

The weather was still summery, although, wherever she went, whatever she did, she felt cold.

Last night she'd returned late to find Vita alone in the kitchen. They'd had a cocoa together and she'd been prepared to linger, half hoping that Vita would give her the opening for confidences. But Vita had suggested she take her drink to bed, as though she were anxious to be rid of her.

Diana had gone upstairs, haunted by the memory of Lee saying, "God help you. You're going to be so lonely." She was discovering that loneliness this minute.

She'd heard Vita coming upstairs. Then there was the sound of Martin's door opening, followed by an urgent, whispered conversation. In the quiet darkness Diana could just hear Martin say, "Did you tell her Lee was here tonight?"

And Vita's response. "Of course not. You know we all promised him not to."

Diana had sat perfectly still, her heart thundering. Lee had been to this house when she was out and asked the others to keep it a secret. After a while she forced herself to rise and made her way to his room. A glance into the empty wardrobe explained his visit.

She returned to her own room, where she sat looking at her phone. It was illogical to think that he might call, but she couldn't help herself. She got into bed, but she couldn't sleep. Coming to the house would make him think of her, and thinking of her might persuade him that they still had a chance. She had to believe there was a chance of that or her heart would break finally.

In those long dark hours she faced the accusations he'd thrown at her. Was it true that she protected her privacy by choosing relationships in which she was the stronger? A review of those she held dear suggested dismayingly that it might be so. Vita and Martin were her pensioners. Clive was more independent, but his poverty forced him to accept her help. Even the animals had all come to her in need.

Lee was a strong man, she argued. But then she recalled their first meeting when she'd mistaken him for a down-and-out. Later he'd been an invalid. Suddenly she knew what it was about her that had always worried him. He was afraid that too much of her love was protective. How could she convince him that he was wrong when she no longer understood herself?

She lay awake all night, watching the phone, willing it to ring, but by morning it was still silent. When she rose she felt as though lead weights were dragging her down, and as she drank her coffee in the kitchen it seemed to her morbid fancy that Vita couldn't meet her eyes.

Now she was wondering how she could get through the day. But the discipline of having to work would buoy her up.

As soon as she reached the courthouse she went in search of the clerk. "I've taken over the case of Alfred Langley at short notice," she explained. "Any chance of rearranging the schedule to give me a little more time?"

He consulted his list. "I can swap you with the theft case, which should give you another hour."

"Thanks. Is my client here?"

"You'll find him downstairs."

She found a waiting room and skimmed through the papers, noting wryly that Langley had a previous conviction. But that could work two ways. An "overzealous" police officer could take previous convictions as the green light to extort a confession by unscrupulous means. She knew Detective Inspector Fredericks fell into that category.

She entered the little cell to find her client waiting for her. He was a youth of about twenty with an open, ingenuous face, who looked as if he could never harm a fly. He rose and offered his hand to Diana. "Hello. I'm Alfred Langley. I can never thank you enough for coming to my rescue," he said.

"Well, let's hope I really do rescue you," Diana said, seating herself and spreading the papers on the table. "Personally I think you'd be wise to apply for an adjournment, even if it does put an end to your holiday."

"Well, actually there's another reason," he said with a touch of awkwardness. "You see I have an alibi, a young woman. We were quite friendly at the time but only because she'd recently separated from her husband. Now she's gone back to him—it's touch and go whether she'll admit that I was with her that evening. She says she will, but I don't want to give her too long to think about it."

"I see. In that case you may be wise." Diana skimmed through the notes again. "What's her name?"

"Lola Daniels."

"I don't seem to have anything about her here."

"She's only recently agreed to stand by me."

There should still have been some mention of a possible alibi in the notes, but it didn't surprise Diana that George had forgotten.

"Look," said Langley with sudden earnestness, "I swear I didn't do it."

"But you already have one previous offense."

He looked at her sharply. "The police can't mention that in court, can they?"

"No, but I'd like to hear about it."

"It was two years ago. I'm not proud of it, and I'm not going to give you any of that it was just youthful high spirits rubbish. I was miserable because my girlfriend had left me. So I drank too much. I was eighteen and didn't handle it very well. While I was drunk I mugged someone. I didn't hurt him, and I got caught almost at once. I've never done anything like it since, but the man who got mugged this time gave a description that was vaguely like me and Fredericks immediately decided he could pin it on me. He was the one who arrested me the first time." He pushed his chair back, looking troubled.

"Go on," Diana said.

"He came around to where I lived and hauled me off to the police station. I said I hadn't done anything, and he grinned in a nasty way and said, 'We'll see, shall we?' He as good as admitted he was going to frame me."

Diana frowned. "I don't think 'We'll see, shall we?' actually amounts to an admission that he was going to frame you. It tends to be one of those vague things policemen say without it meaning very much."

Langley looked hurt. He had big soulful eyes that easily assumed a wounded look. "I thought you were on my side."

"I am on your side, but if I'm to prove police brutality I need something more substantial than that."

"Yes, I know you're right. I'm sorry.

"What did Detective Inspector Fredericks say and do when you got to the police station?"

"Nothing. He got called away as soon as we arrived and I found myself facing another inspector. He was worse. At first he was very subtle. He didn't thump me. Nothing obvious. But he kept me awake all night asking the same questions over and over until I didn't know what I was saying. I wasn't even allowed a cup of tea."

"That's disgraceful," Diana said. "There are rules that say you're entitled to reasonable rest and refreshment."

"There are *supposed* to be rules. You don't think the police take any notice, do you? They laugh at them."

"Not all of them. But some do, I agree."

"I kept asking for that tea. I was dying of thirst. It's incredible how a little thing like a cup of tea can obsess you when you've had nothing to drink for ages. He kept playing cat and mouse with me, pretending it was coming. Only of course it never did. When it finally arrived he wouldn't let me have any. He had one himself, but mine was left on a side table where I could see it. I had to sit and watch him drinking, while my throat was parched. He saw me staring at him and grinned, saying, 'You can have yours when you're a good boy and own up.'

"I went berserk and made a grab at his cup. It fell onto the floor and broke into pieces. He picked one up and—well I'll show you."

Langley took the folder of papers from Diana, thumbed through them until he found what he was looking for, then he held it out to her. Diana's lips tightened at the picture of a hand with an ugly slash across the palm. "He did that?" she asked, scandalized.

"I've still got the scar." Langley showed her his hand. "There's a photostat of my confession in there too. The dark blots are blood. By that time I was scared enough to sign anything."

"But surely there were witnesses?"

"Only while I was signing the confession, not while I was giving it."

"But they will have seen that you were bleeding, and that there was blood on the confession when you signed?"

"Sure. But you don't think they'll admit that, do you? Their story is that the confession was clean at the time and there was an accident afterward. The police will stick together."

"They can try, but that blood is damning," Diana said grimly. "By the way, who took your confession if Fredericks didn't?"

"It was someone with an Italian sounding name. Fortuno, I think. You'll find it among the papers somewhere."

Diana flicked the papers over, moving mechanically. Her ears had registered Lee's name, but her mind couldn't take it in. A part of herself seemed to have become detached and was praying that there had been some mistake. It couldn't be Lee.

But it was. At last she came to the page that she'd skimmed over in her hurry, and there were the words "Detective Inspector Lee Fortuno" staring up at her. "Mr. Langley," she said slowly.

"Alfred," he corrected, giving her a charming smile.

"Alfred, I have to ask you to release me from this case."

"Of course not. We're due in court in half an hour."

"We'll get an adjournment."

"I don't want a damned adjournment. Lola isn't reliable enough to risk it."

"You don't understand. I know Lee Fortuno personally."

The charm faded from his eyes, leaving them cold. "You mean you suddenly think I'm guilty?"

"It's not that. It's that I can't be impartial in the way you need me to be."

"Are you trying to tell me that you're not allowed to cross-examine a policeman that you know personally? That doesn't make any sense. You must be acquainted with most of them by now."

"Acquainted yes, but this was—more than an acquaintance. A defending counsel who was once involved with the chief prosecution witness—surely you can see how dangerous that is?"

"Involved? You mean you're living with him?"

"No."

"But you were?"

"The details aren't important—"

"You said 'was once' involved. Does that mean it's over?"

"Yes, but—"

"Then I've nothing to worry about, have I? I've heard about you. You've got a great reputation for dealing with police brutality."

"And you're not afraid that I'll pull my punches? I wish I shared your confidence."

"If you do, I've got the basis for an appeal, haven't I?"

She stared at him, suddenly seeing the chill calculation that lay beneath the boyish candor. This couldn't be happening. It was a nightmare.

"Do you believe in my innocence?" Langley asked.

"You misunderstand our relationship," she said coldly. "I'm not your judge, I'm your advocate. I'm here to make the best case for you that can be made. I don't have to believe that you *are* innocent, only that you *could* be."

"My blood all over the confession paper is still damning, isn't it?"

"Yes," she said bleakly. "It is."

A policeman looked in. "They're ready for you now."

"Let's go," said Langley. "And don't worry. I know you're going to do a marvelous job for me."

Diana collected her things, then made her way up to the courtroom. Every step seemed to drag, as if she were moving in a bad dream. In a moment she was going to confront Lee, the gentle, caring man whom she loved, and try to prove him a brute and a liar, because that was her job.

More than her job, it was her duty. And Judge Waldman's granddaughter was too good a lawyer to shirk her duty, whatever the personal cost. Her client's freedom depended on her. She had no idea whether he was innocent or guilty, but as she had said to Langley, it was enough that he might be innocent. He was entitled to the best chance she could give him, even if it meant tearing out her own heart and damaging the man she loved in the process.

She tried not to dwell on the thought of Lee's face as she would see it soon, sick with betrayal at what she was doing to him. He would hate her, never knowing that she hated herself a thousand times more. But she would do what she had to, nonetheless.

She sat in court while the formalities were gone through. She saw that the prosecuting counsel was Ted Brand, a stolid lawyer who obtained good results from thoroughness rather than brilliance. As soon as Langley was brought into the dock, the trial began.

Diana listened carefully to the case against Langley, which was a weak one without the confession. In her mind's eye she could see the dark stain on those papers, and her hands clenched painfully at the thought that Lee might be the brute Langley had described. Despite some of the things he had told her about his past career, it was surely impossible. Yet she must try to believe it.

The first on the stand was Inspector Fredericks, who stated with arrogant certainty that the case against Alfred Langley was conclusive. Diana questioned him briefly, managing to make him stumble, but he wasn't the man on which this trial would stand or fall. When Mr. Porter, the victim was called, he insisted that Langley was his attacker, but under Diana's skillful cross-examination he admitted that he hadn't picked him out in the first lineup.

Langley's landlady, a slow-spoken woman with a bovine face, testified that he had been out on the evening in question. But this looked less damning when Diana elicited the information that he was out almost every evening. She finally conceded that she couldn't remember the time in question very clearly, but when Inspector Fredericks had asked about Langley's movements that evening she had replied, "I suppose he must have been out. He always is." This had appeared in her statement as positive certainty, but she'd shrugged and sighed.

Ted Brand rose. "The prosecutions' final witness is Detective Inspector Lee Fortuno."

Diana felt the shock of seeing him again as he entered the court and went to the stand. His eyes flicked automatically over to the defense counsel, and she saw him stiffen as he recognized her. She had the impression that some emotion had rippled across his features like a shadow, then it was gone and his face was a professional mask. With despair Diana recognized that he, too, knew it was her duty to try to destroy him.

Prosecuting counsel asked Lee to describe the obtaining of the confession. Once Lee had begun to speak, he didn't look at Diana but described simply how Langley at first denied any knowledge of the mugging, and then admitted his guilt.

"Inspector," Ted Brand said portentously, "was any force or intimidation used to obtain this confession?"

"None whatsoever," Lee replied quietly.

Diana rose to her feet. "Inspector, are you aware that my client has withdrawn his confession, claiming that he was intimidated into making it?"

"I am." Lee's voice was noncommittal. "But his claim is false, and he knows it. He confessed because he lost his temper."

"Would you explain that, please?"

"He was angry with his victim. That sometimes happens if a mugger is disappointed with his haul. In this case the victim only had a small amount of money on him, and Langley was furious that he was in trouble for such a small gain. I mentioned the heavy bruising on Mr. Porter's face, and Langley said, 'Serves him right for trying to stop me.' Once he realized that he'd given himself away he seemed to lose heart. He shrugged and admitted that he'd done it.''

"At what time did this interrogation begin?"

"Four o'clock in the afternoon."

"And at what time did it end?"

"Just after two in the morning."

"And during that time, was my client allowed any time for rest?"

"There were two breaks of an hour each."

"Are you sure? Search your memory, Inspector. Didn't you keep Mr. Langley talking most of the night without rest or refreshment?"

Lee's mouth twisted in derision. "So that's his story, is it? Well, it was a long night—for all of us. But he was given time to rest, whatever he says."

"And refreshment?"

"He had tea and sandwiches twice. The second time he sent the sandwiches back because they were cheese, which he didn't like. So he got ham instead. We try to provide a good service."

There were titters of appreciative laughter around the courtroom. Lee was making a good impression. "What do you say to his claim that he asked several times to be given tea to drink, and was refused?" Diana persisted.

For the first time Lee seemed to have to search for his answer. Diana's heart almost stopped. Instead of the pleasure she ought to have felt for her client there was only horror.

At last Lee spoke. "He wasn't refused, but there was a hiccup. It was after midnight. We were all tired and in need of something to drink. I sent out for tea, but it didn't arrive. I sent two more messages and still nothing happened so I went to make it myself. There was nothing deliberate about it. It was a lapse in organization. We were short staffed in the early hours."

"It would appear that your services aren't as good as you boast, Inspector," Diana commented wryly.

"Well, we're not aiming to be awarded five stars for hospitality," Lee said drily. "We don't want to encourage people to come back."

There was more friendly laughter. Diana forced herself to ignore it. "So you went to make the tea yourself. Highly commendable," she observed ironically. "I trust Mr. Langley was suitably grateful?"

"Mr. Langley showed his gratitude by breaking the cup and trying to use one of the pieces to slash my face," Lee said simply.

Diana suppressed her instinctive exclamation of horror. Summoning all her willpower she managed to sound lightly skeptical as she asked. "Did you come out of this encounter with any wounds, Inspector?"

"No. I managed to stop him in time."

"Are you aware of the extent of my client's injuries?"

"I'm aware that he cut himself badly, but it was entirely his own fault," Lee said calmly.

Diana hesitated. A hush had fallen over the courtroom, almost as if everyone there knew of her struggle. The silence seemed to stretch on interminably, and she could hear her own heart hammering. At last her head went up. "Inspector, have you ever had a confession dismissed on the grounds of brutality?"

She waited for the look of anger and betrayal as she made use of something he had told her privately. But his face expressed nothing as he replied simply, "Yes."

There was a murmur around the court. Langley looked delighted and sent Diana's thumbs-up sign that she tried to ignore. Brand sighed, failing to mask his wry look. Only the two principals were immobile, facing each other across the court. The air between them electric.

"Would you tell the court about it, please, Inspector?"

Brand rose quickly. "Objection."

"There's no reason why I shouldn't answer that question," Lee said. He looked at Diana. "After all, it's a matter of public record. There was only one occasion. I was questioning a man called Albertson who'd been arrested on suspicion of murdering an old man called Morry Jacobs by kicking his head in. Mrs. Jacobs had witnessed the attack but was too upset and too terrified to identify him positively. But I knew he'd done it, and he knew I knew. He also knew I couldn't prove it. He jeered, not at me, but at the old man he'd killed. I saw red and used my fists. He confessed, but the case was thrown out of court."

Diana heard herself speak as if she were listening to someone else. This wasn't her, attacking the man she loved. It was Judge Waldman's granddaughter, as rigid and scrupulous as the old man who'd taught her everything, and Diana hated her. "And yet you state quite positively that Albertson was guilty. You are, in fact, happy to abuse the processes of the court by asserting his guilt despite his acquittal, knowing that what you say here is privileged. Do you seriously suggest, Inspector, that you are a man whose honor can be relied on?"

"If you mean by that that I can't be sued, that's quite true," Lee replied, unruffled. "But even if I said it outside I doubt if Mr. Albertson could take much action. He's currently serving a life sentence for the murder of *Mrs*. Jacobs. He killed her immediately after he was freed 'Just in case she blabbed,' he said. Luckily this time there were enough independent witnesses.

"A guilty man escaped because of my stupidity, and an innocent woman was murdered. Since that day I've never laid a finger on a suspect again."

A murmur went around the courtroom. Diana knew that it was for Lee and against herself. He'd stood up to her attack, and the spectators were pleased. Some of them were craning to see her face, hoping to discover a look of chagrin. She wondered what they'd say if they knew that she was even more delighted than they. Her spirits had soared with the discovery that Lee was a rock against which she could batter fruitlessly and never harm him, only now that it was too late, she realized how strong he was, strong in a way that liberated her from fear. He would have cared for her as she cared for others, shared her burdens and yet, she had thrown it all away.

They sparred for a little longer, but everyone knew that the crucial question and answer had already been given. When the cross-examination was completed, Lee was still in one piece. It was she who was defeated.

Diana was in two minds whether to put Langley into the witness box, and opened the defense by calling Mrs. Lola Daniels. She was about twenty-five, attractive in a blowsy way, with a smug high-pitched voice. She stated that Alfred Langley had been with her all day and all night on the date in question. She produced details easily without having to think. It was a glib, perfectly rehearsed performance, though all Diana's instincts told her that not a word of it was true.

Ted Brand rose. "Mrs. Daniels, how well do you know Manchester?" he asked unexpectedly.

There was a rustle of surprise in the court. Lola Daniels looked uncomfortable. "Well, I—I've been there," she said at last.

"Until a year ago you lived there, did you not— under the name of Ella Paignton?"

The young woman's smile wavered. "I've never heard that name before."

"I believe you have. Think carefully, please, and remember the penalties for perjury."

Diana looked sharply at Langley, who was scowling in Lola's direction.

Lola licked her lips. "I don't know the name," she repeated defiantly.

"Isn't it true that under the name of Ella Paignton you gave evidence a year ago, in a case in Manchester similar to this? You provided an alibi for a man called Harry Garvie, accused of robbery?"

"N—no." But Lola was looking desperately around her.

"Under cross-examination your evidence was found to be full of inconsistencies, and Garvie was found guilty. The police looked for Ella Paignton to charge her with perjury, but she had vanished. Mrs. Daniels—or Miss Paignton, whichever name you're using now—what did Alfred Langley offer you to provide him with a false alibi?"

Diana leaped to her feet to object, but it was already too late. Lola was sobbing with fear and between sobs was blurting out confused, hysterical accusations about Langley, who had promised her the moon if she'd only "help him out."

The case was effectively over.

Twelve

When the jury retired, Brand strolled over to where Diana was sitting. "Bad luck," he said sympathetically. "It was sheer fluke. I happened to be in the public gallery of that Manchester trial and I recognized Lola Daniels."

"That's life," Diana said with a shrug. "No hard feelings."

"Not that I think you stood much chance anyway. I've seen lawyers break their teeth on Fortuno before. He's as tough as they come."

"Somebody should have warned me," Diana said lightly.

The jury barely deliberated half an hour when it returned and announced a verdict of guilty. Langley looked at Diana and shrugged. They both knew it was a fair verdict.

She gathered up her things, then hurried from the court. She paused in the corridor outside, wondering what would happen now. For once in her life she was confused and indecisive. Then she felt a touch on her arm and turned to find Lee.

Lee hadn't been certain what he would say to her when they met, but when he saw the desperate look in her eyes he knew that nothing mattered except to comfort her. Forgetting their sedate surroundings he bent his head and kissed her gently. She clung to him, half faint with relief. "Lee..." she murmured, "Lee..."

"Hush," he said. "We'll talk later."

"But I need to explain. I had to do it."

He looked shocked. "Of course you had to. I never expected anything else. If you'd failed your client to protect me, I could never have respected you again."

"You mean that?" she asked, hardly daring to believe it.

"My darling, did you think you could hurt me by attacking me in the witness box?"

"I used something you told me in private."

"But as I said, it's in the public record. I hoped you'd understand why I mentioned that."

"You mean—you were sending me a message?"

"I was trying to tell you it was all right. I understood. We're both professionals and we each know what the other's job entails. It would take more than that to hurt me. I'm a tough nut."

"Thank God you are," she said with passionate fervor.

He looked at her searchingly. "Do you mean that?"

"I never meant anything so much. It made me feel—" she searched for the word "—safe."

"Diana, I was going to come and find you today anyway. We have a lot to talk about."

"I know. You came to the house last night, and you told Vita and Martin not to tell me."

"But I only made them promise that because I needed breathing room to work out how to ask you to forgive me," he said quickly. A faint smile touched his mouth. "Did they tell you how they hauled me over the coals?"

"They didn't tell me anything. I overheard them talking. What do you mean—hauled you over the coals?"

"They love you and they've been hurting for you. But they couldn't show it because they were afraid to offend you."

"Oh, Lord," she breathed, "what a fool I've been."

"We both have. They made me feel what a fool *I'd* been, and they didn't pull their punches. Afterward I did a lot of thinking, and I started to see things I should have seen before. I was impatient, wanting our love to give me everything at once, and not understand how much I had to work for it."

Just then, a little crowd surged out the door behind them, buffeting them. "We can't talk here," Lee said, taking her hand. "Let's go home."

They traveled in Lee's car. For the first part of the journey Diana sat with her eyes closed, light-headed with relief at how close she'd come to disaster, and the feeling that Lee's love and generous strength had saved her. The strength had always been there, but she'd blinded herself to it. Only now did she understand how totally she needed Lee to protect her from the isolation that threatened her proud, lonely spirit.

When she opened her eyes she turned to him in surprise. "This isn't the way home."

"It's the way to my home," he said. "We're going there where there are no memories to shadow us."

"But your bed's only big enough for one."

"Good," he said simply.

He parked the car in the garage beneath his apartment building, and they walked to the lift. All the way up to the fifth floor, they held each other, quietly anticipating the sweet moments that lay ahead.

As soon as the front door had closed behind them he drew her into his arms, not kissing her but holding her against his heart. "I love you," he said at last.

"I love you, Lee. Oh, I love you."

"We're both stubborn and awkward in our different ways, but as long as we have our love we'll find a way around that. We'll learn about each other. The only intolerable thing would be to lose you."

"Yes . . . yes . . ." she said, kissing him.

He led her to the bedroom, where they undressed quickly, eager to lie naked together and share reassurance. In the past they'd loved with fierce passion. This time their loving was tender and profound, a giving of the spirit as well as the flesh, bringing them contentment as much as pleasure. Lee's bed was hard and narrow, but in it they found each other again.

Afterward he lay with her cradled in his arms, and she said, "I want to tell you everything."

"You don't have to," he said quickly.

"I truly want to, Lee. You're the only one I could ever tell. But be patient with me. Some of it I've never faced until now."

After that he said nothing, and the silence seemed to stretch on forever, but he wouldn't urge her. She must tell him of her own accord or not at all. Through the contact of their bodies he could feel the terrible struggle going on inside her. He kissed and stroked her tenderly, letting her know that he was at her service, waiting with endless patience for her to be ready.

At last she gave a shuddering sigh and began to speak. "I can see now that neither of my parents ever really had much time for me. They weren't unkind, it was just that there wasn't any room for me in their lives. You saw the pictures of my mother. She was a model, and although she gave it up soon after their marriage her looks were always terribly important to her. It mattered that she should be the belle of every ball.

"I used to overhear a lot of their rows, and I got the feeling that she never really wanted to risk her looks by having children. Grandpa told me once that while she was carrying me my father had an affair, and after that she refused to get pregnant again.

"I was a terrible disappointment to her, not a bit like the dainty little daughter she thought I should be. I looked dreadful in those frilly dresses and I was always asking questions, which she hated. I remember once she snapped at me, 'You'll come to a bad end if you keep asking questions all the time.' Grandpa, who'd happened to be there, glared at her and said, 'That's the stupidest remark I've ever heard.' He despised my mother, and of course she knew it and hated him.

"With my father I was a tomboy because that was what he liked. I adored him. He was away from home a lot on business, so I lived for the days when he came home. I thought of him and me living in a secret world that my mother couldn't enter." Diana's voice faltered as she said this, and Lee held her closer.

At last she went on, "When I was ten years old they divorced. I was sent to live with my grandfather while the upheaval was going on. They said it would only be for a short while. Perhaps they really believed that, and it was only later, when they set up their homes, that they realized neither of them had a place for me. My mother's new husband was younger than her, a bit of a playboy who didn't want a child hampering their life. I think he forced her to choose between us, and she chose him. I'd have been a constant reminder to both of them that she was older than him.

"But the one I minded about most was my father. He didn't marry again at first, and I clung to the hope that he was just waiting until he had a settled home, then he'd reclaim me. When he did marry again, I expected to hear from him every day. But nothing happened."

Diana grew very still as she came to the thing that no one in the world suspected, the memory she could hardly bear to remember, let alone tell. Lee held her against his heart as she forced herself on.

"One day, Grandfather told me my father's wife had given birth to a baby, a boy. That night I slipped out of the house and went to where he lived. I was going to tell him how much I loved him and wanted to be with him. When I reached the house, I looked in at the window. He was there with his wife and the baby. I saw him pick the boy up. He looked at it with an expression of total love and pride that I suddenly realized he'd never worn for me. Then I heard him say—" She broke off, trembling.

"Yes, darling?" Lee whispered. "What did he say?"

Her voice broke. "He said, 'It's wonderful to be a real father at last.'"

"The bastard!" Lee said with soft fury. "Even if he didn't know you were listening—*the lousy bastard*."

She looked up, grateful for his partisanship. He kissed her. "What did you do?"

"I went away. Sometimes I've wondered what would have happened if I'd gone in instead. I know now that he was a man who always took the easy route. He wouldn't have turned me away once I was actually there in his house.

"But I had too much pride. If my life had depended on it I couldn't have told him that I loved him so deeply while he cared so little for me. I went back to Grandpa's house, got in, and returned to bed without anyone knowing I'd been gone. I wanted to cry, but I couldn't. I seemed to have turned to ice. All I could think was how lucky I'd found out before I made a fool of myself. Since then I've always found it hard to cry or to admit when I'm hurt. I've never talked about that night to anyone. I've never let myself face it..."

Her words faded. As her body shook convulsively, Lee felt the scalding hot tears against his skin. He tightened his arms about her and held her, murmuring words of love and tenderness while she sobbed out the pain that was forcing its way to the surface at last. They were the tears of a hurt, rejected child, and he let them flow without trying to staunch them, knowing that they were washing away the last barriers.

Diana sobbed helplessly, feeling Lee's arms firm and comforting around her. At first the tears were a storm that swept over her, leaving her battered. But then came the calm and a wonderful sense of release, as though a great burden had been lifted from her shoulders. The sound of Lee's heart, keeping its slow steady rhythm beneath her ear, seemed to promise her that it would always be so.

"The day we quarreled I was dying inside," she told him. "When you went I wanted to run after you and tell you that you must stay because I needed you. But I couldn't get the words out."

"But you just did," Lee said quietly. Inwardly he was holding his breath.

"Yes, I can say them now because—because I've tried living without you and I can't do it. When I thought of the future without you, it was like looking down into a pit...it scared me. Never leave me. I need you. I shall always need you. Stay with me always."

They were the words Lee had been waiting to hear. He tightened his arms about her, enfolding her in the protective warmth of his love.

"Forever," he promised. "Forever."

* * * * *

SILHOUETTE DESIRE™
presents
AUNT EUGENIA'S TREASURES
by CELESTE HAMILTON

Liz, Cassandra and Maggie are the honored recipients of Aunt Eugenia's heirloom jewels...but Eugenia knows the real prizes are the young women themselves. Read about Aunt Eugenia's quest to find them everlasting love. Each book shines on its own, but together, they're priceless!

Available in December:
THE DIAMOND'S SPARKLE (SD #537)

Altruistic Liz Patterson wants nothing to do with Nathan Hollister, but as the fast-lane PR man tells Liz, love is something he's willing to take *very* slowly.

Available in February:
RUBY FIRE (SD #549)

Impulsive Cassandra Martin returns from her travels... ready to rekindle the flame with the man she never forgot, Daniel O'Grady.

Available in April:
THE HIDDEN PEARL (SD #561)

Cautious Maggie O'Grady comes out of her shell...and glows in the precious warmth of love when brazen Jonah Pendleton moves in next door.

SD-AET-1R

At long last, the books you've been waiting for by one of America's top romance authors!

DIANA PALMER
DUETS

Ten years ago Diana Palmer published her very first romances. Powerful and dramatic, these gripping tales of love are everything you have come to expect from Diana Palmer.

In March, some of these titles will be available again in **DIANA PALMER DUETS**—a special three-book collection. Each book will have two wonderful stories plus an introduction by the author. You won't want to miss them!

Book 1
SWEET ENEMY
LOVE ON TRIAL

Book 2
STORM OVER THE LAKE
TO LOVE AND CHERISH

Book 3
IF WINTER COMES
NOW AND FOREVER

 Silhouette Books®

DP-1